AF572031

RENIFLEUR'S DAUGHTER

RENIFLEUR'S DAUGHTER

Candida Fraze

HENRY HOLT AND COMPANY
New York

Published by Henry Holt and Company, Inc.,
521 Fifth Avenue, New York, New York 10175.
Distributed in Canada by Fitzhenry & Whiteside Limited,
195 Allstate Parkway, Markham, Ontario L3R 4T8.

Library of Congress Cataloging-in-Publication Data
Fraze, Candida.
Renifleur's daughter.
I. Title.
PS3556.R357R4 1987 813'.54 86-26945
ISBN 0-8050-0381-9

First Edition
Designed by Susan Hood
Printed in the United States of America
1 3 5 7 9 10 8 6 4 2

Grateful acknowledgment is made for permission to reprint the quotation from *The Collected Papers of Sigmund Freud*, Volume III, edited by Ernest Jones, M.D., translated by Alix and James Strachey. Copyright © 1959 by Basic Books, Inc., publishers by arrangement with the Hogarth Press Ltd. and The Institute of Psycho-Analysis, London. Reprinted by permission of Basic Books, Inc.

ISBN 0-8050-0381-9

For Peter

PART I

Do not be bewildered by the surfaces; in the depths all becomes law. And those who live the secret wrong and badly (and they are very many), lose it only for themselves and still hand it on, like a sealed letter, without knowing it.

—Rainer Maria Rilke,
On Love and Other Difficulties

1 NEVER COPY

When I was told they were dead, the first thing I did was move into their room. It took all day. The bed was huge and stood so high off the floor that Mama had to use a stool. I took the oak frame apart and carried each piece to the attic separately. Without the bed, the room looked empty. There was only her terra-cotta pot, the size of a small child, filled with roses and buffalo grass. Papa used to say her arrangements were overblown, but to me, at thirteen, they seemed wildly exotic.

Aside from their ark of a bed, that swollen pot was the only other object in a room devoted entirely to pleasure. I was no dummy. Papa came home every day for lunch. He said he came for Lilla's cooking, but I knew better. We all did. It took several days to air out their room.

Spring, summer, and fall afternoons, Papa would walk the five blocks from his chemistry lab at Georgetown University to sit at the glass-top table on the flagstone patio. The sun sparkled through the wisteria vine, my brother Piero toddled around in the grass, and we all had lunch. That part was nice. But after lunch Mama would stretch back in that pretty way she had, and Papa would stand behind her and pull out her chair. "You're looking tired," he'd say. "You should have a nap.

I'll walk you up." And so the two of them would float through the French doors and up the stairs.

What bothered me was the way he commanded her, not so much in words, but by his presence, to stand up and leave the lunch table. The way his large hand slid down her willowy back and around her waist, guiding her inside—her face blank and submissive throughout. It was never clear to me how she felt.

Once I followed, but Papa turned me away at their door. I heard the locks turn and listened for a moment; there was silence, no talking, just a faint sound of rustling clothes and running water. I ran downstairs and into the garden where the mock orange was blooming, and the flowering crab with its pink smell. When I looked up at their open window I saw the white curtains blowing. Strange sounds—little gasps and sighs—fell out the window and into the garden.

It's not that I didn't know about those kinds of things. By a certain age, everyone knew; but they were kept properly furled and private, they weren't made into public events. Our house was different. Mama and Papa claimed all the space and marked it with how they behaved. We knew when and how long; we heard noises; we saw the curtains billowing from their window like some kind of sexual ghost. They were raw silk and most of the year the windows were open and the breezes bellied the curtains like spinnakers, with their lower hems trapped inside. I would stand in the garden looking up. After what seemed an endless time, both curtains would fly free of the window. That's when I started going to Grandpa's anatomy lab—when the curtains got loose and started blowing with each other in the wind, wrapping and twisting around one another. I never stayed around to see them restored to their normal order, to watch Mama pull them back in.

Mama and Papa disappeared on one of their trips to the south of France, where Papa consulted for perfume companies. When their chartered plane went down in the Alps and was never found, I should've felt sad, but I never did—at least not in the right way. I felt relieved. My life was easier without them. Much, much easier. I didn't have to pretend not to notice all the time; I didn't have to make my face quiet and blank when really I felt like shouting, *Stop acting that way, stop giving each other looks all the time in front of my friends, stop going upstairs, as if none of us knew what you did up there.*

My friends' parents didn't act like that. Matt's parents were divorced. Julie's took separate vacations. But my parents just went upstairs. Once I saw Mama's bathroom. Her private things were hanging there—black lace and a kind of peach-colored device with dangles on it. I ran downstairs and into the garden, where I sat on the bench and drew flowers and insects. But it was a wet summer, and by August the garden was dank and rotting. The sweetest blooms were the first to decay. So I abandoned the garden and started going to the lab with Grandpa. He was the Chairman of the Anatomy Department at Georgetown University Medical School.

There were no mysteries at Grandpa's lab, and no deceptive odors. It was a place where things could be safely seen and understood—clean, brightly lit, and permeated with the harsh smell of formalin. Grandpa taught me the word *protocol*—the prescribed way to discover the relations of body parts, how tissues joined, what held things together. It seemed so forthright and honest.

At first Grandpa wouldn't let me help with his work or sit in on his classes. He didn't know I was interested. So I wrapped my legs around the cool metal of a lab stool and colored my flower and insect drawings with the pencils and watercolors that belonged to his medical illustrator, or else looked at plates in anatomy books. When I ran out of drawings to color, I started copying anatomical plates. That got Grandpa's attention. He led me by my wrist into his office and made me sit on his long leather sofa as he paced up and down the room. I was sure I'd done something terribly wrong.

"Never copy," Grandpa intoned. "Never compound someone else's mistakes." His voice was grave. He unlocked the glass bookcase in his office and removed a large leather-bound volume. "This is Tyson." He held up the book. "*The Anatomy of a Pygmie*. He was the first evolutionist. One hundred years before Darwin. 1699." He turned pages. "He was brilliant," Grandpa muttered. "Here," he said. "Listen to this: '*My chief design is the improvement of the Natural History of Animals; which is better written from Nature's Own Copy, than the faulty transcripts of her many Commentators.*'"

He closed the book and peered over his glasses at me. "Do you understand? Never copy. Draw from life."

From that day on, Grandpa started giving me things to do. I would help his lab assistant, erasing and washing blackboards, finding slides, distributing mimeographed sheets before class. He gave me the keys to the specimen case, and I could draw whatever I found inside.

2 SECRETS

For a long time it bothered me that I didn't seem to care about Mama and Papa. At first I thought I didn't care because I never saw them dead. Seeing people dead made you really believe. A casket with the actual body, right there, got put in the ground. I'd been to funerals before with our housekeeper, Lilla. I saw her niece, Cynthie Lee, just six, all dolled up in dotted swiss and white patent shoes and even some rouge on her chocolatey cheeks, her hair done up in dozens of braids, each one with a white barrette, and her nails immaculate, not the way they were when we scrabbled in my playhouse under the lilacs. She died of what Lilla called "Smilin' Mighty Jesus," and it was years before I realized she was saying "spinal meningitis."

Our lives didn't change much when Mama and Papa died. We stayed in the same corner brick house at Thirty-fourth and Q streets in Georgetown. Grandpa gave up his apartment and moved in. It was his house anyway. He had given it over to Mama and Papa when my older sister Prima was born. I never wondered, until much later, about Grandpa's wife—who or where she was. Grandpa was complete in himself. I couldn't imagine him as part of a couple.

Clipper and Lilla stayed on in the carriage house in the back and kept on doing what they'd always done: Clipper the garden, Lilla the house. Prima went back to college. It was her freshman year. Before she left, I asked how she felt about Mama and Papa. I wanted her to be more like Mama, as nice as she was pretty. Instead, she delivered one of her withering looks, and said, "What do you *think* I feel?" After that she never talked to me much, and when she did, it was only to make me feel stupid for not understanding whatever it was she understood. Prima the Princess, that's what I called her behind her back. She never chattered or cried, and her sharp eyes saw us and judged us, as if she weren't a part of the family. She would fix me with her hard stare. "You're a liar," she'd say. "You belong to the night. You creep around silently, poking your nose where it doesn't belong. You're a dark person." I felt condemned. I was glad when she went back to school.

Piero was too young to say much. Lilla had been raising him anyway. He kept going to the church nursery school around the corner. Lilla asked me to go through Mama's things, but I said no, and they disappeared to the attic with everything else, leaving behind just what I wanted: no memories, no mysteries, no trace of who they had been.

When I was younger I'd liked exploring in Mama's grown-up secrets. I liked her dresser the most: its curved rosewood drawers, and the nougat-patterned marble top, which felt cool and smooth to my hand. An oval mirror rose like a bright sail, straight to the ceiling. I loved the scent of her mingled perfumes; she had dozens of bottles ranging across the back of the dresser, like spires against the mirror. One of her drawers was filled with carefully folded silk scarves. Another held a silver box with Botticelli's *Primavera* in bas-relief on the lid. It held her collection of "beautiful things": unstrung pearls, a single fiery opal, the crystal drops from an old chandelier, and antique buttons sewn onto a strip of black velvet so soft she called it "baby skin."

Tucked away in her dressing alcove was a lady's desk of burled wood with spindly legs. Mama told me it had been her mother's—the only piece she'd brought from home. It was there that she wrote her endless letters to Aunt Noel, her spidery handwriting filling sheet after sheet of thin blue watermarked paper. Aunt Noel was Mama's sister, five years older, who lived in Paris. Mama called her a free spirit. Papa said she was a rebel. All I knew was that when Noel came, and brought the man she lived with in Paris, Mama became gay and funny and laughed all the time. She gave parties for Noel and they stayed up late and drank bottles of wine and Mama saved me the corks. But after a while Noel came alone. I was never told why, but once I heard Noel and Mama talking. Papa didn't like another man in the house, Noel said, and a young handsome Frenchman at that. Mama didn't answer either yes or no, so I never knew what she thought. But soon after that, Noel stopped coming. Instead, she wrote to Mama, and every week, Mama wrote back. I came to recognize Noel's handwriting, her india ink, the French stamps, and Mama's preoccupation after a letter arrived. When Mama wasn't writing to Noel, she did her real work, her translating, downstairs in the library, or else next door with Mr. Sylvester, over endless cups of tea.

Mr. Sylvester was unlike any other adult I knew. "Monsieur Sylvester," as Mama called him, spent his mornings reading in his second-floor library. Papa would sometimes invite him for lunch, but he was always "engaged," which made Papa smile, I didn't know why. Without fail, Mr. Sylvester would leave around one, and wouldn't return until late afternoon, when he often invited Mama for tea. Evenings found him at embassy receptions and theater parties. He was Swiss, and owned a chocolate-manufacturing business that had been in his family for four generations; but "Monsieur Sylvester" never worked at his business the way Papa and Grandpa worked at their labs. Apparently it wasn't expected. Mama said it was because he was a gentleman, and I knew by the way she said it that she approved. Mr. Sylvester spoke French and Italian and shared her passion for translating Dante. No one spoke about Madame Sylvester; she didn't exist. But Charles did. He was Mr. Sylvester's son.

Charles changed our lives. I met him for the first time on an evening in June. He had just come to live with his father. I was seven, barefoot in the grass, hoping for a glimpse of the first fireflies. A boy with long dark hair and a black cape was standing behind the wrought-iron gate that separated our garden from his, next door. He gestured to me. I walked tentatively to the gate. He whispered through the bars, "What's your name?"

I told him my name was Mona. He whispered back that if I opened the gate, he'd show me a trick.

"Wait," I said, and ran to find Clipper, who kept our key. When the gate swung open, Charles strode into our garden, took three yellow balls from a drawstring bag, and began to juggle. Could it be that he was a real magician?

Charles became our leader immediately, not because he was the oldest boy, or the tallest, or even because he had an endless supply of miniature bittersweet chocolate bars, which none of us liked; we were used to gritty Hersheys. Charles became our leader because he seemed immune to our family drama. He hadn't been watching Mama and Papa, as the rest of us had, trying to make sense of how they behaved, or looking for a way to fit in their world. He had games of his own that he wanted to play, and he couldn't be bothered with grown-up charades.

Charles was eleven, Prima's age. Matt Wallace was the only other child on the block. He was nine and had adopted himself into our family. On summer mornings, right after breakfast, Matt arrived and stayed through dinner. Before

Charles came, I couldn't see what Matt found so attractive, or why he preferred our house to his own.

Charles, Prima, Mona, and Matt. The four of us huddled together under the latticed thicket of lilac which was to be our clubhouse, and Charles intoned the solemn words: "Oday ouyay eakspay igpay atinlay?" The others laughed delightedly and said, "Esyay, esyay, eway eakspay igpay atinlay!!"

It took me three days to realize that pig latin wasn't an actual language, spoken in some remote African country. I had to learn. They were all fluent. Even Matt.

Charles called our club the Quartet. He said it meant a group of four, playing together. I liked that idea. Our first assignment was to map our gardens: paths, gates, and trees were located, benches and walls marked, escape routes identified—everything plotted in minute detail. Charles said if we had a good map, we could bury treasure, like Long John Silver in *Treasure Island*. On that first afternoon, as we were rushing around in the garden with pencils and paper and measuring tapes, a sudden cry flew down from the upstairs window. It was Mama's voice.

"No!" she said. And again, "*No!*"—much louder. Then silence. Absolute silence.

I stood rooted to the grass. Charles was beside me. He twisted his mouth in disdain, and then, to my horror, he shouted back up at the window: "*No* to you too! *No, no, NO!*" There was silence from the open window. He turned to me. "Forget them," he said, and pulled me off to continue our project. But I couldn't forget. Mama never raised her voice. I didn't know she had the power. There was something about the way she held her exquisite body, a kind of purposeful quiet, a stillness, a carefully balanced poise, as if she were in a state of continuous abeyance. She only seemed to come alive when she was writing letters to Aunt Noel, her head bent in intense thought, feelings rippling across her face, her eyes cloudy, or bright with tears, or filled with shadows. Or else, when she was working with Mr. Sylvester, chattering, laughing, all animation.

Later that same afternoon, Papa appeared, his white shirt blazing and his dark hair damp from a shower and slicked back. He was on his way back to work. He stopped and stood over Charles, who was using the garden bench as a table to draw our map. He stood so close I could smell the starch on his shirt.

Charles felt his shadow and stood. At eleven he was already tall for his age. They were two dark men, facing each other.

Papa's voice was icy. He stared at Charles. "Did you have something to say to me?"

Charles ran a hand through his long hair and widened his eyes. "Good afternoon, sir." He opened his arms and gestured. "We're trying to mark where everything is."

Papa's eyes glittered at Charles, and Charles returned his stare with a steady gaze.

There was a long silence. Finally, Papa said, "I see." Then he said, "You're quite a young man, aren't you?" and, without waiting for a reply, walked abruptly away.

Charles turned to me, grinning, and said, "*That's* what you learn in boarding school."

About an hour later, Mama came out to sit in the garden. She looked the same as she always did, nothing peculiar, nothing at odds. It was clear I had misunderstood.

Our club had a secret greeting, a password, and a code that Charles devised using the telephone dial. Our refreshments were stolen from one kitchen or another. Especially prized were sourballs from a jar Lilla kept hidden high on the pantry shelf, and which she sucked to keep from chewing tobacco.

In the fall we collected bushel baskets of magnolia pods from the tree in Charles's garden, and pine cones from the tree in the alley, both of which became ammunition for attacks we launched at Grandpa when he came over for dinner, or at Charles's father on his way out to parties. Charles wanted to ambush Papa too, as he walked back and forth for his lunchtime visits, but I begged him, please no, it wouldn't be wise to draw Papa's attention.

Papa's attention was unnerving. He was especially conscious of anything female. His eyes inspected and appraised each tiny detail. He noticed what women wore, how they arranged their hair, how they smelled, and how they walked. He noticed hands and feet. He not only noticed; he had opinions. We had all heard his views on suntanned skin and synthetic perfume.

But most of all, Papa noticed Mama. "You're looking wan today," he would say, and sure enough, under her pool-blue eyes was the barest smudge of a violet shadow. He would reach over and run his thumb under her eyes, then curve the palm of his hand across her cheek and rest it around the back of her neck. "Perhaps you'd best not work today," he would say, his eyes holding hers. When he looked at Mama, his gaze was thick and electric. When I first saw a picture of the sculpture *Laocoön*, I thought of my parents: twisted and bound to one another in some strange, intense, primordial grasp.

3 THE GOLDEN BOX

One day Charles walked into our garden carrying a golden box, heavily embossed with geometric patterns. It looked like one of the Magi's gifts in a Christmas play. He held the box above our heads.

"This," he said, "is a secret treasure."

"What is it?" I cried, leaping around him to reach the box. While Matt and I begged him to open it, Prima stood to the side, watching.

"No," Charles said, his broad grin going suddenly solemn. "You must each guess." He handed us slips of paper, and with pencil stubs that we kept in an old orange-juice can in our clubhouse, we wrote our secret wishes and dreams. I imagined a romance of my own, just like my parents', as golden and shiny as the mysterious box. Prima wrote that inside the box was a small island where she lived, all by herself. It was real, she said, a dream that she had every night. We were so different.

Charles never opened the box. How did he know, at such a young age, that it was more interesting to imagine than to know? That a closed box was more mysterious and entrancing than any object it could possibly hold? Charles had power. With him, I felt safe, brave enough to imagine a life of my own.

In the winters, after school, when we knew Lilla was busy with dinner and wouldn't disturb us, we put on plays or magic shows. Matt and I were trolls and devils, servants and messengers. No one questioned that Charles was the hero. And Prima the princess. Or, when we played sardines, that Prima was always "it," and that, every time, Charles found her first, leaving Matt and me wandering around in the creaky silence, holding hands and trembling with fear as we peered under beds and opened closet doors. We could never find them, and inevitably, when we had to call "All-in-free, all-in-free," they would appear out of nowhere—Prima rumpled and flushed, and Charles looking smug. We stamped our feet. "You cheated. We looked everywhere!" Charles combed his dark forelock back with his fingers. They had been in the guest-room closet, of course. "You weren't! You weren't! We looked there." Charles shrugged. Matt and I looked at each other. How clever he was, he always fooled us. Charles was our leader. We never thought to doubt his word.

But Lilla did. In early May, at the beginning of our third summer together, she complained to Mama. Seasons were changing and Mama was making one of her rare forays into the kitchen. I peeked through the door and saw Lilla's hands on her hips, which was always a bad sign.

"Mrs. Emory, Matt's going to camp this summer."

I was horrified. Did Matt know? I wondered.

Mama looked up and smiled—a bright but wholly distant smile, as if she were facing an audience. She lifted the lid of a crock and peered inside. "What's this?" she asked.

Lilla ignored her. "Day camp, in McLean, Virginia."

Mama dipped her finger into the sugar. "You don't think swimming and the library are enough?"

"Not for Miss Prima."

"What *can* you mean? Prima is a young lady."

"Yes, ma'am, exactly that. Thirteen years old."

"Hmm," said Mama. She looked up at Lilla and delivered another of her brilliant, glazed smiles and said, "I'll take it up with Dr. Emory. Will that do?"

I heard Lilla say, "Loose ends ain't nothing but trouble."

Mama nodded her head gravely and sailed out of the kitchen.

The next thing I knew, there was a pronouncement at dinner: "Children, your father and I have decided to send you to camp. I have gathered a list of suitable places; we'll visit this Saturday morning. Then we'll decide."

"But Mama," I said, "Piero's only three. He can't go to camp."

"Of course not. But you're nine and Prima's thirteen—perfect for camp. Here's a place that offers riding; perhaps you'd like to learn to ride? Do you like horses?" Her question was plaintive. She looked vaguely hopeful and bright-eyed. It was obviously an effort for her to put herself inside anything so quotidian. I had the feeling she was floating thirty feet above us. Problems like camp and summertime and being out of sugar required an unaccustomed focusing of attention.

After one disastrous summer of camp, we learned to preempt Mama and Lilla. The next spring, by the time the camp brochures were stacked beside our breakfast plates, our plans had been made.

"Oh, no, Mama," Prima said firmly. "I'm taking a biology course at St. Albans summer school. It will take all my time." She waved an application form and pressed Mama to sign on the line.

Mama was nonplussed. Before she could catch her breath, I chimed in, "Mama, I'm busy too. Matt and I are going to the lab. Grandpa said we could." She looked perplexed. "You seem so young for the lab, I know you've been going. . . ." Her voice trailed off.

I was ten. Anything was better than camp, or hanging around in the garden, watching those curtains blow out the window. After two blissful years of loose ends, with Charles as our leader, everything changed. Mama was using words like *structure* and *supervision*, and each Friday at dinner she asked about our plans for the weekend. We quickly learned it was wise to have them. To avoid being trotted off to every imaginable organized activity—ballet, piano, sewing, Girl Scouts—we had to look busy and stay out of reach.

At the same time, Mama was spending more time at her upstairs desk, writing letters and keeping her journal. And Papa dropped in at odd hours, not just for lunch, and brought work in a briefcase to do at home. He and Mama had long talks behind closed doors.

During all these upheavals and changes, Prima became a boarding student at Madeira School in Virginia, and at the same time, Charles disappeared—with no explanation—at least to us. The Sylvesters simply moved away. It was a day in early fall. Prima had already left for boarding school. I saw a moving van outside the Sylvesters' house, its open maw devouring piece after piece of familiar furniture. The gross proportions of the truck looked obscene on our block of Georgetown houses. In shock, I went outside and stood by the curb, waiting for Charles to come out and explain—or at least to sneak over and say his goodbyes.

He never did; he had left with his father the week before. He dropped out of our lives, as quickly and as mysteriously as he had dropped in, which made me wonder if our club and our games had actually happened. Or were they a dream? He moved away and never wrote. Not one letter.

Later, when I could compare the events, I knew that Charles's leaving was worse than Mama and Papa's dying. That was how I felt. Our lives changed more dramatically then. There was no more running back and forth through the open gate in the brick wall that separated our garden from his; there were no more plays in our basement, with old bedspreads for curtains. No more spying games or treasure hunts with maps and clues written in code.

I missed having a second home; I missed knowing that Mama and Mr. Sylvester were having tea, talking and reading snatches of poems, conversing together in French and Italian, their sibilant whispers a constant hum as we raced up and down the long, carpeted stairs in Charles's house, stealing butter cookies from their tea tray to take to our secret garden hideout.

But most of all, I missed having a life of my own—childish wishes and secret plans, perhaps, for romance—which, with Charles as protector, seemed perfectly safe and served as a distraction from Mama and Papa's lunchtime dance through the French doors, up the stairs, and into their bedroom.

With Charles there, we knew we could cope with Mama's plans; with Prima being away—she'd come home for the weekends; with our parents' disturbing charade. But with Charles gone, we couldn't continue our games; we weren't the same, and, even worse, we'd lost our power. I stopped dreaming about a life of my own and felt myself being pulled back into orbit around Mama and Papa, like a pale moon whose only role was to witness their heat and reflect their glow.

Piero was too young to feel the loss, but the rest of us had to have new distractions. Prima's solution was school; she became a serious student. At seventeen she was admitted to Radcliffe. The same year, I started going to Grandpa's lab not just in the summer, as I'd been doing before, but every day after school and on weekends as well. It was relief almost verging on pleasure. I felt safe at Grandpa's lab, learning what I needed to know. There were no words, no looks, and no moving parts—and no meanings, other than those prescribed by Grandpa. There was only the harsh anesthetic of formalin, covering everything over. By the time Mama and Papa died, a year later, Grandpa's lab had become a habit. A way of life.

4 PAPA

Children don't always have words for what they know. In this way, although we lived under my parents' spell, even after they died, we never discussed them. It was what we did that showed their power.

When I first started going to the lab, as a way of avoiding home and camp, Matt followed along. There was no question of leaving him home. Officially, he lived across the street and down one block, but unofficially, he lived with us. Matt was an only child, and he said we seemed like his real family. Lilla routinely set a place for him at dinner, and even later, when we weren't so small, Grandpa grouped us together, calling us "the diminutives," the little ones—Piero, Matt, and me—as usual using five syllables to say what he meant, when two would've done fine.

At the lab, Matt listened patiently to Grandpa quoting Tyson and haranguing about four thousand years of anatomical misinformation; he sat quietly as Grandpa repeated stories we'd heard several times before—that Leonardo was the first to show the correct curvature of the spine, the correct position of the fetus *in utero*. But the truth was, Matt didn't like gross anatomy. The body didn't explain what he wanted to know. He liked to think about the world at a different level; he was curious about the absolute insides and inner workings of things. In high school, when he was learning physics, I teased him about loving empty space, those vast distances between electrons. I said he was making things smaller and smaller. But Grandpa told me to leave him be. Someday, he said, Matt would have a lab of his own. Grandpa and Matt were very good friends.

Matt was tall, with dirty-blond hair, and skin stretched taut over a bony face. He ran track in high school and played the drums in a band after school. He carried his drumsticks with him everywhere, rattling and tapping and beating out rhythms on whatever objects presented themselves: tabletops, flowerpots, benches, bus stops. He was always around—to help me with algebra problems or Clipper with something heavy that had to be moved. He loved to sit at our kitchen table, especially in winter, when Lilla baked cookies and casseroles. Our house smelled like a home, and he liked that.

Matt taught himself to make fudge. He would cook it to the soft-ball stage, and pour it onto a white ironstone plate: a smooth puddle, just up to the interior rim. What a shiny brown eye it made, a perfect circle of glossy enamel. When Matt made fudge, it meant things were okay between us. Even when it turned out grainy and hard, which often happened, making fudge was a way of saying what couldn't be said, a kind of confirmation with sugar.

Matt's father was a one-term congressman who had stayed on as a lobbyist when he wasn't reelected. He lived on Capitol Hill. Matt lived with his mother in a house that smelled of lavender-scented paste wax—an odd combination of sweet and petroleum—and was full of Queen Anne furniture and heavy damask draperies. The curtains were never opened and the rooms were more to walk through than to live in, lifeless and empty and always quiet, like a small museum that's very familiar. When I went there, we spent most of our time in the kitchen or on the screen porch, both of which were sunny and old-fashioned. If Matt wasn't stirring up fudge, there was always a wooden case of Cokes under the kitchen sink, and no one to tell us not to drink them. There were no rules at Matt's house.

But even as we sat swilling contentedly from soft green bottles, we knew the Cokes had a high price. They were there because of Matt's mother, or "poor Miz Louise," as Lilla called her. "Miz Louise" would drift into the kitchen or onto the porch, wherever we were sitting, lift her hand out of the voluminous folds of her silk kimono, and shade her eyes with her thumb and fingers. "Why, you sweet things," she would say, "surely you want some refreshment—now just you wait, I'll phone the store right this minute." In spite of our protests—there was plenty of Coke—off she would drift and soon we would hear the click and whir of the telephone dial in the front hall, and then the murmur of her soft Georgia voice. Next thing we knew, the delivery truck from Pearson's would pull up to the house and Matt would wince as the man carried in a cardboard carton, or sometimes two, of Jim Beam or Jack Daniel's, and finally, as an afterthought, a wooden case of green-bottled Cokes.

My house was different. We had lots of rules and Papa was the acknowledged arbiter of everything. The entire household revolved around his demands. He dictated the time of dinner and the menus and the wines. He demanded that we dress, if not formally, at least in clean clothes, and Prima and I had to wear dresses, never pants. I can't smell shoe polish without thinking of Papa. We couldn't be scuffy or down-at-the-heels. We had to be ironed, starched, buttoned, and brushed. No dirty nails, no mulberry stains from the tree in Charles's yard, no rips from crawling through hedges or holes. Immaculate. Why? He didn't give a damn what anyone thought, that wasn't it. So why did he care about how we dressed?

He said it was to distinguish us from animals. "No other difference," he'd mutter. "Animals with clothes on." If we were human, we should distinguish ourselves from lower forms. We should express our elevated evolutionary status with the artifacts and accoutrements of culture: perfume, coiffure, clothes, and, above all, style. Food was not only nutrition and fuel, it was part of our aroma. Our diet was bland and slightly Southern—no garlic, curry, or spices, and not too much butter or fish. Clipper wasn't to grow any vegetables in the broccoli family, or onions, turnips, cabbages, or radishes; they overwhelmed the natural human spoor. Papa wanted us pure.

Eating was not a practical matter. It was an aesthetic event. Linen, silver, china, and most of all—time. No rushing, no piling everything on one plate. Everything we ate was served as a separate course. He said it was to make us learn to delectate, to make the eating a sensuous act.

Clothing was not protection; it was adornment. A house was not shelter; it was enchanted and fabulous, draped and crusted with beautiful things. Their bedroom was not a place to sleep, but a private bower.

Our yard was not a yard. Papa wouldn't use the word. It was a *garden*—a textured, scented place of refreshment, a stage set for his outdoor scenes with Mama, and a laboratory of scented plants.

Papa liked to grow plants that defied the climate: waxy camellias, which he grew under glass; gardenias, which he grew for the scent; and pots of jasmine, which were carted outside in the summer to grow on a trellis, and back inside in the winter. He made no accommodation to climate. The climate had to adjust to him.

Papa had opinions on all subjects. Not opinions—his

views were beliefs. He had a way of making them indisputable, of surrounding them with a shield of truth.

He convinced us all. Who were we to challenge his judgments about apples or architecture or the right wattage of bulbs for reading? His supreme self-confidence did us in. He made us feel that he had arrived at his beliefs after deliberate consideration, and that all the world, were it sensible, would surely agree. Where did he get that manner? Was he, underneath all that surety, a puddle of ambivalence and querulousness, like the rest of us? Did his confidence disguise a profound doubt? About what? Or was he simply glib and bright and verbal, forming his opinions as the words were being formed in his mouth, his tongue moving from the soft to the hard palate, from the back of his teeth to the top, taking its orders from a brain that raced like an engine gunning in neutral gear? I never knew. He was an actor who never broke character.

Even though Grandpa owned the house, Papa forbade him to smoke his pipe when he came over for dinner. "My nose is my livelihood," Papa said. "Smelling is my business; you must not pollute my olfactory processes."

He could talk like that and no one would laugh. Papa was a research chemist. His lab was on the university campus, but he took government contracts and consulted for private companies as well. His specialty was odors, scents, pheromones, esters. He collected smells, studied them, and tried to make them synthetically. He said smells were the key to control; memories, feelings, old desires—he said they were all released by smell.

Papa said he "had a nose." That was different, he said, from "*being* a nose." The sense of smell decreased with age, he said, so a real nose would have started an apprenticeship at fourteen. He was just a novice. But to us he seemed terribly fussy.

He wouldn't go into the vault at the bank when Mama needed to get her jewels; he said he could smell the dirt on the money, and besides, he complained, the bank was next door to a Chinese restaurant, and he hated the odors of garlic and ginger, the smell of soy sauce.

When we were walking downtown, visiting museums, he could smell a fountain blocks away. He would stop short, his expression intent. "Can't you smell the water?" Sure enough, a few blocks closer, we'd detect a bloom of dampness, a faint trace-odor of chlorine.

Papa wouldn't come with us to the beach. He said it smelled like rancid oil and white sugar, with a Coppertone top note. So for two weeks each summer Grandpa took us to Matt's parents' beach house at Rehoboth Beach. Mama was never allowed to come. Papa said she'd come home smelling like a waitress.

Papa complained to Grandpa, his own father, that he came over for dinner stinking of formalin. "You know what it does," he said. "Of course you know. It's not just a preservative, it deadens your sense of smell; it anesthetizes the olfactory bulb. How can you do that to yourself?" Grandpa just smiled and went out on the porch to smoke his pipe.

Papa smelled rain, and snow too. He could smell fear, he said, and certain diseases: the fruity breath of a diabetic, the musty odor of liver failure. He could smell a dieting woman; he said her breath had ketones in it, a faintly rotten smell. Humans had six odors, he said. When he told me that, I put my face to my arm and inhaled deeply. I was faintly sweaty, that was all I could smell. Papa ran his nose up my arm. "You're musky," he said. "You smell like me." I was shocked. It wasn't possible. Papa's broad shoulders were always encased in a suit; he smelled only of starch and dry cleaning. Occasionally, when he took off his suit coat and rolled up his sleeves to consult with Clipper in the garden, I was disturbed to see his long white muscular arms and the faint sheen of sweat on his face.

He taught us the perfumer's vocabulary: top note, base note, aldehyde lift, and explained how to create an *accord*—using fixatives and scents with different volatilities.

One day he took me outside and we waded into a pile of oak leaves mounded in the gutter.

"Smell," he said. "What do you smell?"

"Dryness?"

"Dry decay—a sort of embalming. A lovely smell."

"What about burning leaves?" I asked. "Can you make that smell in the lab?"

He didn't answer. Burning leaves were a sore point with Papa. The city had passed an ordinance making open fires illegal, and Papa was outraged. He said it was like taking cinnamon out of Christmas, or the odor of damp ashes from a summer fireplace.

Papa never told us what smells he was trying to create at his lab, but for a while I was sure he was studying something at home. He took to hanging around when Lilla was washing, but she wouldn't have it. I saw her standing at the laundry-room door, talking to Papa and holding her broom across the threshold like a lance. She would not let him in. If olfaction was Papa's domain, the laundry belonged exclusively to Lilla. She soaked, rolled, sprinkled, and boiled; she made the whites blaze like a vision. And then she starched. Heavy, light, and polishing starch. Clear starch for lace curtains and collars. Her starching was a sanctifying ceremony; she seemed to think it would give us an uprightness we didn't have, or couldn't acquire in any other way.

5 THEIR GRAND ROMANCE

"What you have is an Oedipal problem." Julie turned the pages of Hunter's *Gravid Uterus* as she spoke. "Who cares if they're dead? You can still be jealous."

I was in high school. Julie was my best girlfriend. Charles was forgotten. But forgetting my parents wasn't so simple. Julie and I had been reading Freud—Papa's standard Strachey edition, twenty-four blue-covered volumes, crammed with secrets, clues, and evidence. We read about wet dreams and guilt; about puberty rites and German nannies molesting their charges. With Freud as our text, Grandpa's collection of anatomy books provided the graphics.

In our library foraging, we found a facsimile edition of Leonardo's anatomical drawings, and in it a picture we longed to see: a longitudinal cross section of human intercourse—a swollen penis tucked firmly inside a vagina. The torsos were standing with the legs arranged to permit penetration, which was something we were both curious about.

"Listen," Julie said, "this can't be real. You can't do it standing up."

"Who says?" I was staring at the picture. He must've imagined this scene, it was something no one could actually see—an interior view.

"I suppose if the people are about the same height," she said, fingering the corner of the page.

"Of course it's possible," I said. "Sitting, too. Sitting on his lap." I had thought about this a lot. I was staring at the folio pages, wishing some other artist had done this scene instead of Leonardo. He was too classical; his accuracy was almost clinical. There was no feeling. I thought of other early anatomists: the *Commentaries* of Mondino, Estienne's weird scribbles, even some of Casserius's plates. I liked their primitive rudeness, their ignorant distortion. I was fascinated with inaccuracy in anatomy, with error and mistake. Confusion about the body seemed to add feeling, to make the drawings themselves more expressive. In my mind, a picture of intercourse should be drawn in a mannerist style: exaggerated and contorted, with lurid colors and dramatic light.

In contrast with what I wanted, Leonardo's picture wasn't remotely suggestive—no heads or hands, not even the legs. Even more peculiar, the veins and arteries from the genitalia were extended to the heart, to show the source of engorgement, I supposed. It was what I imagined that made it exciting—a romance like Mama and Papa's, fully illustrated—and then, peculiarly, very depressing. Mama and Papa were my only standard: their bodies, their conduct, what they'd liked and disliked. Although I'd never know what they'd actually done, I did know, at the very least, that I looked nothing like Mama. Her face had had topography: a straight, perfect nose, a tiny pointed chin, and large, round, deep-set eyes with delicate brows arched over them. She'd been as blond as a peach and as full of details as a miniature porcelain shepherdess, and even worse, Prima looked just like her—fine-boned and delicately articulated, with a tiny waist, full breasts, and a tight, round bottom. In contrast, my body was all of a piece. Its parts flowed together—breasts, waist, hips, thighs—in a lean line, from top to bottom. I would never have Mama's hourglass figure, the way Prima did. I was deeply ashamed. Papa must have disliked my body. I felt animal rather than human. That the phone rang with invitations to go bowling and then to Howard Johnson's, or even to Chevy Chase Club dances, made no difference.

Papa had intrigued everyone. He was handsome like an old-fashioned soldier: tall and fair-skinned, with smooth black hair and a black mustache. His facial bones were flat and rounded, like worn-down mountains, and his nose snubbed, not the least like Mama's peaks and hollows.

Papa knew everything. Especially about Mama. He even chose her perfumes. She had scents for every season and time of day. In the morning she used something clean and powdery-smelling, but nothing so obvious as citrus, nothing green. Later in the day she wore a single floral top note—perhaps carnation or rose. In the evening when they were going out, I remember Mama standing at the bottom of the stairs, beautifully draped and smelling of musky, complex scents, and Papa's long-fingered hands cupping her face, his large thumb rubbing the side of her cheek, and Mama, eyes closed, lowering her face and tilting her head to rub against his persistent hand.

In the summer she wore jasmine. I couldn't smell it without thinking of her—of both of them. Their emanations tinctured my life.

Papa was always bringing her presents. He would arrive with a fat camellia, or a spray of yellow freesias, or even an orchid. When they went out at night, she twisted his flowers into her hair. Once he came home with a small box with a red seal on it. It was a pair of earrings with miniature urns hanging on gold filigree chains. He filled the small urns with perfume, and when she moved her head, the perfume drenched her bare shoulders with scent. He gave her a huge carnelian brooch, with the head of Medusa carved in high relief. It was he who gave her the enormous terra-cotta pot in their bedroom, and a collection of silk scarves in the palest colors: apricot, June blue, maize, sea green.

When Prima and I were little, we would creep into Mama's dressing room, drop our cotton shorts and T-shirts in a ragged heap on the floor, and drape ourselves with her finery: silk scarves, long satin ribbons, lace collars, and embroidered shawls. We unfolded her stockings and tied them up with ribbons or scarves. By wearing her beautiful things, we would be beautiful too. After all, these were things that Papa had chosen. But many times, instead of feeling like the bride or princess I dreamed of being, I felt uneasy. I thought I was wicked to want to be Mama.

Plumed and draped, we would float downstairs to the large front room, where we rolled up the scattered Oriental rugs, pushed back the chairs, and put Ravel's *Bolero* on the record player. We adored the drums, the wailing horns, the steady, inevitable increase in tempo—and most of all we loved the unbearable waiting. Leaping, spinning, whirling in circles, we tried our best to devise a choreography for the mounting crescendo of the music. As the pace became faster, and the beat and rhythm correspondingly insistent, we made higher leaps and faster turns—and that, of course, was when Lilla appeared.

She marched to the record player and lifted the stylus, ignoring our rage. "Get upstairs and dress yourselves. You got five minutes to be out in that yard." She stood with her huge arms folded over her starched bosom and glared at us as we drooped up the stairs. We sighed and wilted. We were no longer glamorous, floating, romantic. We were damp and bedraggled, our scarves rumpled, our hair stringing around our faces, our cheeks pale behind febrile spots of color. We had been caught, not so much in the act, but before its consummation.

For some girls it was horses. For me it was dance. But Papa didn't like bare feet and leotards and what he called "orgiastic acting-out." He preferred ballet: curtseying to the dance mistress before each class; hair pulled back in a tight bun from faces pale and taut with effort; bound feet and a stiff tutu. The vanity, the posing, the comparisons of leg extensions and turnouts—that was acceptable.

Did Lilla report to Papa about our displays? I was sure she did. I was frightened and deeply ashamed. I felt something amiss, something shadowed and not entirely clean. It wasn't that Papa would say anything—I knew he wouldn't. It was that he would *know*. But *what* would he know? Was it about me? Did he know what I wanted?

It was their attachment I wanted, their strong feelings, their grand romance, all of which felt foreign to me. Bodies by themselves didn't have much meaning for me. From my work in the lab, I knew how bodies looked and were put together. I knew what was supposed to happen—which was why I liked Freud and Margaret Mead; they gave the body emotional weight, gave meaning and feeling to physical acts.

"Who wouldn't be jealous?" said Julie. I had told her about the lace and linen, the silk curtains, the urn of flowers; about Mama's perfumes, the starch in the laundry room, the avenues of clean sheets being hung to dry in the laundry yard—white, unblemished, pristine sheets. Their bed was changed every day.

I had felt excluded, I told Julie. I still did. My family had not been like other families. In other families the children came first, not because they were loved more, but simply because they were dependent creatures, because they were *children*. In our family, my parents' love for each other came first. I could never compete with their calculated hedonism, with the good taste of their voluptuousness, with the aesthetics of their love for one another. And as far as Papa was concerned, there was nothing more unfashionable than a baby. Piero was clearly unplanned. After he arrived, Papa sulked and moped. He said Piero didn't smell like our family. He wouldn't hold him or play with him or show him off proudly like a normal father. Being a father of girls was fine, or at least tolerable. But who had asked for another child, and then—what gall!—a boy-child? A rival. Strangely enough, Matt felt the same way. He was used to being the boy in our house—an adopted son and Grandpa's friend. He stayed away after Piero was born. When Grandpa came over for dinner, as he did at least twice a week, I complained about Matt's disappearance. I was six and Matt was my only friend. Charles wouldn't arrive until the following year. On his way back to his apartment that evening, Grandpa paid a call at Matt's house. The next morning, Matt appeared at the door, as if nothing had happened. But he and Piero were never great friends.

Papa forced Mama and Piero to move into the guest room, and he took over the bedroom suite. He couldn't stand the smell of a lactating woman. Poor Mama. She was the one who needed to be resting in the silky quiet of the bedroom, the sun filtering through the white curtains, the cool shadowiness of it, the dreamlike quality. But no. He claimed it. He took it for himself, and demanded dinner on trays and pots of tea. He competed not so much with Piero as with Mama. He complained that he was ill, that something terrible would happen and he would never, ever, see Mama again.

Finally, Papa demanded that Mama stop nursing. Piero was eight weeks old. Soon after that, Charles came to stay with his father, and Mama and Papa left on the first of their many trips—to Greece, to North Africa, to the south of France—all for Papa's researches.

Julie poked me. "Kevin isn't bad," she said.

"Ugh." I wrinkled my nose. "He smells like peanut butter."

"What about Ron Packard?"

"Pimples," I said.

"Not on his hands."

I sighed. Julie was a pragmatist. "It's not the same," I said. "I can do that myself. I want—"

"I know, I know." She smiled and nodded. "You want 'luuuve.' The real thing." She rolled her eyes back into her head, then snapped her head down and peered into my face. "Right?"

"I don't want this sticky phase—ten minutes tangled up in the back of Ron Packard's souped-up Ford."

She shrugged.

Okay, I told myself. There's something I don't want to admit. I'm a jealous person. And envious, too. I can't compete. I can't be like Mama was, or even like Prima. I'll never, ever, find someone like Papa.

6 CENTERFOLD

In 1969, ours must have been the only house in Georgetown without air conditioners. Grandpa didn't want them. After spending all day in chilly, formalin-drenched air, he craved open windows and natural temperatures, regardless of the heat. Unlike Papa, Grandpa kept most of his rules at the lab, and was benign and slightly abstracted at home, letting Clipper and Lilla manage the house. It seemed the least we could do to honor his wish. We had to make do with awnings and fans, and closing the house against the sun.

It was a sticky June afternoon, and Piero and I had walked to the barbershop for his regulation summer haircut—extra-short to keep him cool in the heat. While Piero clambered into the barber's chair, I slouched on a vinyl sofa, its chrome arms greasy with fingerprints, and picked up a magazine from the floor. It was *Playboy*. I flipped through the pages until I came to the centerfold, which I turned vertically for the full effect. I stared at the breasts. They were full globes, the nipples erect, the aureoles a blushing pink. The flesh in the picture appeared smooth and uniform—no hair, no sags, no lumps or scars. I ran the palm of my hand over the page, trying to equate the satiny texture of the paper with the skin it portrayed. I looked up at Mr. Finzio, who had started to cut Piero's hair, and then peered down the front of my T-shirt.

Mine were not magazine breasts. I remembered Prima's gloating words—*Mona is olive-complected*—as if I'd been pickled like one of Grandpa's cadavers. I stared at the page. Surely these were ideal. I studied them. They'd been retouched with an airbrush, of course, and with smug satisfaction I noticed the slackness of the pectoralis major.

Mr. Finzio looked up from his cutting and glared, first with surprise and then with disapproval. He wanted me to watch TV or cross over to Sugar's drugstore for a Coke. But I didn't care what he wanted. These breasts were important—not these in particular, of course—but the idea of living flesh. I looked at Mr. Finzio blankly, seeing not him, but the middle distance, a place of consideration and imagining. I'd had enough of drawing dead tissue, of the careful description of fasciae and tendons, layers of muscle, the bones of the hand. I was eighteen. I'd graduated from high school and would go to Bryn Mawr in the fall. I needed to learn what everyone knew: the surface of things.

He was standing on a dais, changing his pose every sixty seconds. The teacher called for a long pose and the model turned to face the class, one leg in front of the other, one arm up, the other curved beside his body, like Michelangelo's *David*. Except for the scratch of charcoal, and the slight movements of students looking up at the model and then down to their paper, over and over, the room was quiet.

Was I the first to notice? First it wobbled. Then it rose, slowly, like an arm, parallel to the floor, then higher until it was pointing obliquely toward the ceiling.

I stopped working. How odd, really, to have a naked man standing in front of me, his penis pointing mysteriously toward the skylight. I looked around the studio to see if anyone else had noticed. Was this a common occurrence? Something to ignore? Or did it merit—what could it merit? I had no idea. Should the model put his hand down and caress himself until he felt better? Should one of the students go over and do it for him? How did one cope with the random urges and callings of the body? How could these things be controlled? Should they be? Of course they should, but it was difficult in a roomful of students, half of them women. Was that the problem? I looked around quickly, counting four men, who seemed not to have noticed. Or perhaps they were practiced at hiding their feelings. I was embarrassed, but didn't know why. From my time in the lab, I knew male bodies. After years of giving Piero baths, I knew that even little boys had erections.

The teacher called a break. He went up and draped the model with a cape, his arm solicitous and protective. There was a rustle of papers, a scraping of stools, the beginning of small talk. Several students went out the louvered swinging doors for coffee downstairs.

Bodies that moved, bodies that could get up and walk away, bodies that were still young and working—these were a new drawing experience. The teacher had been reluctant at first; he had wanted me to start with the beginning class. At which point I brought out my portfolio. It wasn't much, just sketches I'd done for Grandpa's articles, some cross sections and a bird's-eye view of the pelvic girdle. He looked carefully at the drawings, one by one. Then he looked up. "Okay," he said, and initialed my form.

I had expected questions about why I did anatomical renderings, and had come prepared with plausible answers. But he didn't ask. He stared out his window in silence until I realized with chagrin that I had been dismissed. He didn't care about *what* I had drawn, just *how* I had drawn it. It was I who cared. At the registrar's office, I asked for the class schedule. While other students were marching against the war, or being teargassed just a few blocks away, I would be spending three hours a day, Mondays through Fridays for six weeks—half of June and all of July—in another room without an air conditioner. It was going to be a sticky summer.

7 LOOSE ENDS

Not all the classes were as dramatic as the first, but it took most of the summer to learn a new way of seeing. The aliveness was disturbing. Nothing held still. Muscles rippled, legs and arms altered shape with every slight shift or rotation. When I had a position fixed, the pose would change—the leg would flex, the arm extend—and I would have to start over. For the first two weeks I was unable to finish a drawing. I was learning a different view. Instead of my usual meticulous drafting, I learned to make impressionistic sketches, which were still more literal and accurate than anyone else's. The other students were here to learn anatomy. With me it was the reverse.

I complained bitterly all summer. I complained to Grandpa, who complained back that he missed me in the lab. I complained to Piero, who, at twelve, didn't understand, but listened soberly and attentively anyway, his large eyes solemnly fixed on mine. I should quit, he told me, or perhaps I should practice at home. He would model, he said. Piero was full of solutions, even then. All I wanted was sympathy. I wanted someone to understand my discomfort.

When I complained to Matt, who was home from his sophomore year at Johns Hopkins and working in a lab at NIH, he listened too, with a certain tolerant amusement, like an older brother, and when I was through moaning and groaning, he took me for walks across Wisconsin Avenue and into Montrose Park. We would stare through the twilight at the huge tulip poplar and beech trees, and into the deepening shadows. When the streetlights blinked on, we would start the walk home, and occasionally stop on Wisconsin Avenue to eat enormous bowls of ice cream, and then continue slowly along the cobbled brick sidewalks in the summer dark.

"I'm going to Italy in August," Matt said, on one of our walks. "Why don't you come? You graduated. You deserve a vacation. You can see the real thing—Michelangelo, Bernini. Also," he added, "you can avoid the demonstrations."

Neither of us was involved in the culture of protest. Each summer, as floods of students and demonstrators streamed through the streets, we simply continued business as usual. It wasn't that we disagreed with their goals, or even with their methods. It was living in Washington. For years we'd been reading the *Washington Post* and watching the antics of politicians; it was impossible to see the political process as anything but obtuse and self-serving. But besides these complaints, both Matt and I felt uncomfortable with ideas that weren't scientific. We wanted control. Politics was amorphous and fuzzy. It didn't attract us.

I stared into the dark. "It would make a change," I said. I spoke as if talking to myself. I looked over at him.

Matt got off the low brick wall where we were sitting. "Think about it. My project is finished in two weeks. I'm flying to Venice."

"I want to visit Grasse," I said. "You know, in the south of France." The words came out before I could think. What did they mean? My parents were in Grasse before they died. What did I think I would find there?

Matt ignored me, as he always did when I talked about anything other than matters of fact. "I don't care where we start," he said. "We could fly to Paris and drive down. Come on, let's go. I'll speak to Grandpa."

"He'll think it's a great idea." I could feel Matt grinning in the dark. I knuckled his shoulder. "A conspiracy, that's what it is."

"A conspiracy to do what?"

"I wish I knew." I hopped off the wall and dusted my skirt. My class was almost over. High school was finished. Until college began in the fall, I was at loose ends.

With the warm dark silting around us, I looked over at Matt, striding along beside me. We had played together for years. We had witnessed, with combined horror and fascination, my parents' dramatics, his mother's drinking, his father's absence. We had shared the loss, first of Charles, and then of my parents. We had vacationed at Rehoboth Beach with Grandpa, had walked back and forth from school and the lab, reeking equally of formalin; we had shared specimens, colds, fudge, gloves, and houses. I knew what Matt liked to eat, what made him cross, how he behaved when he was hungry or tired, what he liked to read, the clothes he wore—and he knew the same facts about me. But with all this, we never talked. There was nothing to say that the other didn't already know. We had the kind of involuntary intimacy common to siblings, a visceral closeness, not developed from discussion, talk, or conscious efforts at understanding, but from being together day after day, year after year. Matt was my partner in games, my conspirator in knowing and not knowing, an adopted older brother with whom everything was shared. It would be perfectly logical to travel together.

8 ENFLEURAGE

I wrote to Aunt Noel in Paris. Could Matt and I come for a visit? Could we stay with her in her Paris apartment?

A telegram came in reply: ALWAYS WELCOME. LOVE, NONNIE.

But Paris was empty when we arrived. As we walked into the gloomy black-and-white-tiled lobby of Noel's apartment building—bleary-eyed from our flight and laden with bags and a bunch of flowers from the Orly vendor—a stooped man emerged from the shadows and handed me a letter. We put down our bags and flowers and cameras, and stood under a dusty chandelier to read the letter.

Darlings—

It's all yours. I'm in Cannes—above it, actually, in a small villa, where you must come when you're finished with Paris. Help yourselves to everything, and ask Girard if you have any problems. He only looks like a troll—it's part of his job to be fierce. You'll find everything you need in my desk: maps and guidebooks and a list of restaurants. I'm used to visitors! I use the café on the corner a lot, it's called Micromoulin, the food is good and inexpensive. . . .

I stopped reading. After almost ten years, Noel had become a mythic figure. She had written, of course, and sent occasional presents, but I wanted to see her again. I had no current image to which I could fix my memories.

In that grim period after Prima went to boarding school and Charles left, I had spent hours in our old clubhouse under the tunnel of lilac branches. By midsummer I had tramped down whatever grass there was, and carried out my special treasures: my pixie marbles, my real china tea set, and the books that Aunt Noel had sent from Paris. She wrote a continuing series of popular children's books, about a miniature, secret, hidden world. Her books gave me just what I needed: a private, controllable life. I loved her for that.

Inside my small green room in the lilacs, with a latticelike screen of branches between me and the world, I plotted my future and nursed my griefs: I would be a famous dancer when I grew up, the modern kind, with bare feet and clingy leotards, and live in Paris like my Aunt Noel. And I would *not* be proper. When Aunt Noel had stopped visiting, I was sure it was Papa's fault. He didn't like her. After every visit, Papa would sigh and say gravely to Mama, "Your sister is *not* a lady." What did it mean to be a lady? Was Mama a lady? Would I be a lady? What did he want?

So we stayed by ourselves, rattling around in Noel's Left Bank apartment—four spacious, high-ceilinged rooms full of watery light and pale, fragile French furniture. The tables had thin, coltlike legs, and were finished in a wash of white and gold; the settees and chairs were upholstered in faded pastel-striped satins, both shabby and elegant, and unlike anything I had seen before. Was this family furniture? Was this what Mama had had as a child? Her father had been a cultural attaché in the foreign service, and had been stationed in Paris and Florence when she and Noel were young. When they'd lived in Paris, Noel had liked it so much she decided to stay there for school. After that, she had never left. Mama said she was smart. It was a better place to live in the fifties, she said. I looked again at Noel's Second Empire furniture, and then thought of the solid Victorian chairs in the Georgetown house, the huge rectangular golden oak dining table, the carved and encrusted headboard on my parents' bed. How staid and lumpish they seemed next to these gazellelike pieces. For the first time I wondered how my mother had felt about using someone else's furniture—about using someone else's *everything*, in fact. Even their house had belonged to Grandpa first.

We lasted a week. I had come with a vision of nineteenth-century Paris—crowded cafés and black umbrellas and beautiful women wearing lots of perfume. Instead of Degas and Utrillo, I was presented with de Chirico: an empty stage set. Plazas, boulevards, cafés—all were virtually deserted. Paris in August was eerie, and not the landscape I had in mind. I wanted something more conventional and distracting, hustle and bustle, a working city.

But still, I felt obliged—both to Matt and to Paris. We went to the Jeu de Paume and to the Louvre and to the Tuileries. We took pictures of one another under the Arc de Triomphe. One morning we got up early and went to Les Halles, only to discover it had been replaced with something sterile in glass and steel. No garlic soup and wine at sunrise with Parisian workers. Where was the Paris we had visualized? Every conversation we overheard was in English or German. Tourists were everywhere. We had our pockets picked going up the elevator in the Eiffel Tower and bought perfume for Lilla and for Matt's mother on the Champs Elysée. But all this time, I was secretly bored and, even worse, unaccountably tired.

Noel's apartment was in the Latin Quarter; its windows looked out onto a narrow street lined with shabby stuccoed shops, a restaurant or two, and other apartment buildings.

When I wasn't napping, I spent my time sitting on the tiny wrought-iron balcony that opened off Noel's living room, sipping Cinzano and staring blankly into the street. I couldn't remember the last time I hadn't been working. My life at home was an unquestioned routine, reassuring in its sameness. After school, and during vacations, I went to Grandpa's lab. If nothing else, I was always busy. Except for trips to the beach with Grandpa, which always seemed vaguely medicinal—we were "taking the waters"—this was my first real vacation.

"We need to get out of this heat," I said. "We can go to the country too."

Matt demurred. He wanted to go to Longchamps, to Montparnasse, to Les Invalides. He was the better tourist. He felt more obliged to be one. But finally I convinced him. We picked up a rental car and headed south, through Chartres, through the Loire Valley, reading our *Guide Michelin* and stopping erratically to see anything rated *vaut le voyage* or marked with three stars. I was still exhausted. Chateau or charnel house, I couldn't care less. I stopped only to start again, as if my job were to stay in motion and to log miles.

In Grasse we toured the perfume factories; we watched trays of lavender flowers being placed on sheets of wax. It's called *enfleurage*, I told Matt. Papa had taught me.

"I know it's crazy," I said to Matt, "but I wanted to see where my parents had been."

He looked at me reflectively.

"This is the last place they were seen—before they flew from Nice and their plane went down. I thought I would find some sign, something. . . ."

I didn't feel sad, just rueful. No matter how often I tried to explain it away, I was haunted by the recurrent image of my parents—their eyes locked, my father's hands, my mother in voile, her light hair a cloud of wisps in the damp summer air, and finally, their carefully choreographed dance through the French doors and up the stairs. They were my only vision of how to conduct an adult life, a life in the world. I wanted to see them through grown-up eyes. I wanted to learn their patterns. To join the world.

9 FOUNTAINS AND GARDENS

From Grasse, we went to Noel's villa. It was in the hills above Cannes, its red-tiled roof set snugly into the hillside, its stuccoed stone the same buff color as the landscape. Low stone walls gathered the terraced land into strips and oddly shaped rectangles, with groves of olive trees and small vineyards lacing the hillsides in orderly rows.

Dogs began to bark as we drove up, and Noel appeared, framed in her low doorway, waving us in. She was a tiny woman, and was wearing wide-legged black cotton pants and a loosely woven shirt of the same material. Her long, silvery hair was held up in a French twist with tortoiseshell combs. She was elegant, even on vacation. She welcomed us into a cool, open foyer, with terra-cotta tiles and rough, white stuccoed walls. She led the way up three steps and down a sunny hall, its windows overlooking an interior courtyard. We were given connecting rooms with a bathroom between, and Noel suggested we meet in a hour for lunch. It was all more formal than I had expected.

I had expected to be hugged like a child. I had expected Noel to look the way she had stayed in my memory: a double of my mother, just as beautiful and magical, but slightly more vivid. But here was Noel, with silver hair, not really old but not young either, a successful author of children's books, sophisticated, confident, and certainly not my mother. This Noel had had serial lovers. And had stopped visiting. Or had she been banned?

We stayed three days. We took walks in the olive groves and on the terraced hills; we visited pottery factories and Picasso's studios and had elegant lunches in small cafés in Vence. Noel was polite and charming and asked dozens of questions. Mostly, Matt answered. I wanted to ask questions myself, but never had the right words. On our last day, as we were standing by the car, I blurted out, "Noel, what happened? Why did you stop coming to Washington?"

Noel looked surprised and then sighed. "Your mother never told you." It was a statement rather than a question. "Wait," she said, and disappeared inside. After a few minutes she reappeared with a package wrapped in brown paper.

"Please don't give me a present," I said. "I feel terrible, we arrived empty-handed, we—"

"It's not a present," she said. "They belong to you." Noel smiled. "At least now they do."

I started to unwrap string and brown paper.

"Save them," she said, putting her hands over mine. "They're your mother's letters."

"Oh." Disappointment was clear in my voice. I had wanted something just for me, a personal thing, like the children's books Noel used to send, the books with her private miniature world. Quite suddenly, I didn't want any actual possession of Mama's, anything real that would remind me of how different we were from one another, and of what I wanted—which was to be like her. I kissed Noel and managed my thank-yous. Matt shook hands. In the car, I handed the package to Matt and he tossed it into the backseat. We drove until lunch without speaking.

Just past the Italian border, we stopped to buy lunch supplies before the shops closed for the afternoon. Grapes, a slice of ricotta, and two hard rolls. Matt bought bottled water to wash the grapes, and some local wine in a terra-cotta flask. We drove into the hills, with spectacular views of the sea and the town flashing left and right as we hairpinned up the hillside.

Matt was too quiet. I couldn't remember his being like this before, silent and tense. I thought I knew him. He liked pecan pie and Ross Macdonald mystery stories. He liked Chekhov plays and particle physics. He was good friends with Grandpa. When something heavy had to be moved, he was there, on the other side of it, helping Clipper. Matt was tall and American-looking, with a little boy's face gone all bony in adolescence, his eyes a light, watery blue. There was nothing difficult or mysterious about him. An angry Matt wasn't someone I knew. Finally he spoke.

"We need an agenda."

I didn't understand.

"What do we know? How can we decide between Turin and Bologna? All we know is . . ." He paused.

I laughed. "All I know is how to work."

"Exactly." He grinned. "We have to make this work."

"It already is."

He stopped smiling.

"Well, you must admit—"

"Not my fault," he shot back.

"Are we fighting?" I said.

He gave me a hard look. "The royal 'we' are trying not to fight."

"La-de-da!"

"Mona. Give us a break."

He was right, of course. Neither of us was particularly good at not having something to do. Touring around and "having a good time"—as we had been urged to do by Grandpa and Piero as they waved us onto the plane at

Dulles—was not something at which we'd had much practice. So. An agenda. I couldn't think.

"But really," I said, "I'm tired of work."

Matt looked at me. He sighed. He took the water bottle from my hand. We had finished lunch and were lying in the grass beside the road. "I don't mean your real work. I mean we have to make something up. We have to decide to take a picture of every free-standing equestrian statue in northern Italy, or every Tuscan garden; we'll get out the *Michelin* and make an itinerary and when we *get* to the free-standing statue or garden, I will take your picture in front of it—and that will be *that*." He bounced a grape off my head.

"I get it," I said.

"Good," Matt said. "Do you agree?"

"About what?"

"Jesus! What's the matter with you?"

"Nothing's the matter. Of course I agree. I said that."

"Okay, good." He folded his arms behind his head and looked at the clouds mattressed above us. It was a rare gray day. "What shall we collect?"

"You just said." I threw a pebble at him. "Free-standing statues and Tuscan gardens."

"Not big on decisions, are you?"

"Not *at all* big on decisions. But very grateful if someone else is." I bit my lip. "Matt, I'm sorry."

"Uncle." He broke off a long stem of grass. He rolled over. "How about fountains, but only ones in piazzas and central squares, places like that?"

"I liked the gardens."

He didn't care. "Okay," he said. "Fountains and gardens. Let's make a plan." He opened the guidebook.

10 THE AGENDA

Genoa, Pisa, Florence, Ravenna. Then finally Venice. Matt's plan worked. My mysterious expectations vanished. I stopped feeling tired. Our agenda became a marvelous game: posing and clowning and taking each other's pictures in front of tiny village wells, or else with river gods and water nymphs in enormous baroque wedding-cake fountains.

We became the way I imagined we should be: pals, friends, traveling companions. No permissions had to be asked or granted; neither of us had to pretend to be polite, we could say and do whatever we wanted, and were simply glad to keep each other company and stay out of trouble. Since we knew each other in the familiar, undemanding way of friends who hadn't yet learned how fragile friendship was, we enjoyed each other with blithe indifference. We didn't know enough about anything, especially history, to understand what we were looking at, but we were equally uninterested in the same things.

In spite of our ignorance, we began to judge and classify places: by the sculpture, by the interior spaces, by the public squares and qualities of light. I loved cart paths and cobbled alleys, old and new buildings jumbled together, the way a narrow, shadowed street would turn a corner into a sunny, immaculate, paved piazza.

As we traveled from fountain to fountain, from garden to garden, what had started as a blatant device to structure our time became, instead, a special way of being together.

But Venice was different. It took us by surprise and changed everything.

Before Venice, we had avoided beaches. I hadn't even packed a bathing suit. But in Venice, water was everywhere; it was the medium of existence. It defined the environment, controlled the light and the weather and the smell of the place. Very soon we knew that we couldn't just ride around on the water, we had to get *into* it—swim in it, play in it, be in and part of the water. We went to the Lido beach.

I bought a bathing suit that was nothing like the chaste Cole of California creations I wore at home, with built-in bras and modest skirts. It was lavender, what there was of it. I tried adjusting my breasts into the tiny triangles provided to contain them. They were like melons at the top of a full string bag.

"You'll be assaulted," Matt said.

"Everyone wears them."

"What's this scar?" He touched my back.

"A mole. Benign."

"Oh."

Our eyes met. I could tell he was thinking something. Solving some problem. Matt was like that: rational, efficient. At every level a problem-solver. When he talked about school and work, he said there were only two interesting subjects to think about. Physics and the brain. He thought the brain was too difficult; he would stick with physics. I thought he'd end up a doctor—perhaps in research.

Matt stared at my body the way he might assess a specimen at the lab.

"You're beautiful," he said.

I blushed.

"Let's swim," he said.

We swam, but everything was different. For the first time I thought of his body, tall and blond and wedge-shaped. What was wrong with me? Mama had had Papa. Matt was for me. It was that simple. All this time he'd been under my nose. Too close to see. Available, attractive, a known entity.

A known entity. That's what had made me discount him. But it shouldn't have. I looked at him. What did love mean, anyway? I'd always thought it meant shivery feelings and crashes of thunder and trailing around the house with a slightly blank expression, like Mama. But maybe it wasn't always like that. Maybe people could choose love. Could I choose Matt? At least I could try. I kept looking at him.

We played in the water. It was opaque and pale, a dull mirror, and warm, like bathwater.

"Will you sleep with me?" I asked.

Matt was floating on his back. He kept floating, his eyes closed. "First time?" he asked.

"Yes."

"What if you don't like it?"

"Isn't that unlikely?"

"Just suppose."

"We can stop." I was floating beside him. "Can't we?"

"A little awkward," he said.

"You haven't answered." I put my hands on his stomach and pushed him underwater. When he came up I was standing, the water just above my waist. He swam up and stood behind me, very close, his bare chest touching my back.

"It will change things."

I turned my head to look at him. "How?"

"It just will."

"What else? Precautions?"

"That's easy. Didn't you just have your period?"

"How did you know?"

He touched his nose.

"Bad?"

"Not at all. Just distinctive."

He looked away from me, squinting at the sky. It was one of those overcast days, but very warm, with an even, white light. "The first person is very important." He seemed to be talking out loud to himself. He turned back to me.

"Are you saying you don't want to?"

"I've been thinking about it since Paris."

"Why didn't you say something?"

"I was waiting for you to wake up."

"Oh."

He nodded.

"I'm awake," I said.

He gave me a long look. He put the flat of his hand on my flank. "We'll make the best of it. Two beginners."

"You too?" I was surprised.

"No." He looked back toward the shore. "But this is different."

I wasn't sure what he meant by *different*. I thought he meant we would have time. It wouldn't be a matter of creeping around in the backs of cars or waiting for an empty house. We swam some more. It was decided. Everything with Matt was like that.

11 VENICE

I went to Florio's and bought an expensive bone-handled manicure set, carefully folded into a smooth, fawn-colored leather case, and then, back in our room, I manicured Matt's fingers and toes, elaborately and slowly. I examined his ears and proclaimed them perfect. I studied his profile, his posture, the bones in his face, and how he parted his hair. I watched the shift of his flesh as we lay in bed with the warm afternoon sun flooding in the windows. I ran my hands over his flanks, his buttocks. His chest was smooth and hairless. I combed his hair, cleaned his ears with tiny Italian Q-Tips, and peered for long stretches at the foreskin of his uncircumcised penis. When I took it into the palm of my hand, it stirred slightly. I lay down and placed it between my lips.

Matt laughed and called me a baby.

I loved the aliveness of his body, the feel of warm flesh. I loved being able to watch it move, change, do work, perform. I loved being a part of its action. I was astonished to find feeling embedded in flesh. He reminded me that skin was an organ.

I bought creams at the *farmacia* and rubbed him until he was smooth and scented and thick with readiness.

Matt said I was drunk.

I said it was the light.

Matt said I was perverse, but he smiled when he said it.

It's the water, I said.

Matt said he wished he'd known. He would have taken me swimming before.

Matt told me later he'd been looking at me that way for over a year and had begun to despair that I'd ever notice. He said Grandpa knew, Prima knew, everyone knew—it was a family joke. When he told me that, for a brief moment I hated him, hated them all.

I told him I wanted to go to art school instead of Bryn Mawr. To someplace close to Johns Hopkins.

Matt said I'd better watch out.

Why? I asked. Watch out for what?

Matt never said. He just turned and pushed me down.

12 DELUGE

All that water, the color of ax blades, and shiny in the same dull way, its texture smooth like the inside of a cheek. It was receiving water, as if it would swallow whatever fell in, and close over it.

I threw my old self into the water and it sank like a stone, as if my previous life had never existed and would never be missed.

The water absorbed us and transformed us. It washed into our hotel rooms, over our beds, into our eyes and veins and pores, and out again. We were flooded with sensation, awash in a frictionless, buoyant, amniotic merging. Air, water, light, and horizon blurred into a damp, rich mist, in which we drifted without definition. We fused with each other and the place. There was no existence in apartness—no will, no self, no intention. Neither of us moved without the other. Our chemistries flowed together so often and so completely that our scents mixed; we were olfactory twins, a blend of honey and musk, our own perfume, with Venice the base note.

13 A ROMANCE OF MY OWN

The balcony of our hotel room overlooked the Grand Canal, and we spent hours watching the comings and goings of boats, listening to the swish of paddles and oars, the buzz of motors, the click and thump of wood against stone. I had been reading *Macbeth*.

"Sound and fury, signifying nothing," I said, waving my arms to the world at large. The balcony inspired dramatics. I wanted to remind myself that this wasn't real, that this wasn't the life we had at home. Matt would be a junior at Johns Hopkins. I would be starting Bryn Mawr as a freshman. How would it work? I wanted to hear what Matt had to say. So I said it again. "Sound and fury, signifying nothing." It was clearly a challenge. Matt jumped off the bed where he was lying.

"Don't say that. You know it's untrue." He stood beside me, looking out.

"What's untrue?"

"'Signifying nothing.' That's existential blather. It signifies if you say it does!"

"What do you mean by 'it'?" I said, looking ingenuous.

"You know damn well what 'it' is." He turned to me and took me by the shoulders. "Don't play games."

"But I'm in good company." I waved the book. "Shakespeare believed it."

"You're in good company right here, with me."

"Angry company."

"I don't like your doing one thing and saying another. I just had my hands all over you. You were whimpering, you cried out, you called my name, you begged me. We spent one hour in that bed"—he gestured back to the rumpled sheets—"giving each other exquisite pleasure, and I won't hear you say 'signifying nothing.'"

I was silent. I knew he was right.

"I love you," he said.

"Is that what 'it' signifies?"

"Yes."

"But what does your loving me mean?"

He glanced at me, a look of sadness and rage on his face. It made me shiver.

"That's the hard part," he said.

"What's hard about it?"

"Never mind." He gestured again to the room. "This is real. It exists. It's not 'nothing.'"

I needed to know how he felt because I couldn't say I loved him until he said so first. I was that unsure. I had surrendered my body, was swamped in sensation, and Matt was responsible. I needed him; he created my feelings. And what were those feelings?

With Matt, my boundaries dissolved. I was tightrope-walking, holding myself on a wire of sensation, carefully easing myself across, pushing myself to a place of complete submission. Afterward, I was blank, wrung out, in a state of dreamy remoteness.

I would give up anything for Matt, for his hands on my body. It was the only thing I cared about.

Was this the romance my parents had had? If so, it was

happening to me. Matt and I were like Mama and Papa. I felt released and relieved. I'd arrived.

I hadn't thought of my parents in weeks. Quite suddenly, I remembered Mama's letters as well—the brown-paper-wrapped package from Noel. Where were they? I was curious. Had Mama's romance really been as wonderful as mine was? I was sure the letters would tell.

I asked Matt where they were. For a moment he looked perplexed. He was lying on the bed, his head propped on his hand. "Oh, yeah," he said in a muffled voice. "*Those* letters."

He was sorry, he said. He'd sent them home in the large package we'd mailed a few days before. We were inexperienced packers and hadn't thought to leave space for things we'd buy—guidebooks, perfume, bathing suits, aluminum vials of lavender in Grasse, pottery in Venice, the usual hodgepodge of souvenirs. So Matt had packed up the clothes we no longer needed and sent them cheaply, by boat, to Baltimore. I hadn't known he'd put in the letters. I'd forgotten them completely.

Matt apologized again, but I didn't care. It was what wanting to read them meant. It meant I felt equal. I had a romance of my own.

14 MATT'S LETTER

We left Venice. Matt hated hosteling, and so, on our drive back to Paris, we stayed in private hotels with spectacular views of mountains and lakes. In the mornings we went out because we felt obliged. We took photographs, ate impatient lunches, and then hurried back to our rooms. We emerged at sunset, starving.

We had a week of this. Then a flight home. Matt drove me to Bryn Mawr in his old gray '54 Ford, and then drove back to Washington. A few days later he took a train to Johns Hopkins. I spent orientation week studying a map and the college guide, looking for an art school close to Baltimore. I would transfer after my first semester. I would bide my time. I was sure we would marry. And then Matt's letter came.

Dear Mona,

I'm writing instead of inviting you up because if you were here we'd spend the weekend in bed, and nothing that needed saying would get said. I can just hear you saying, What's wrong with that? *And the answer is, Nothing, of course, you know how I feel. But there is something wrong.*

I can't seem to keep you as the person you were—the person I grew up with, the person I like as well as love. Something's happened. I've changed you. I imagine that I won't be enough. That you're florid with need. That you'll go with anyone. I make you into someone you're not.

When I imagine you talking to other men, I'm sick with jealousy.

You're completely naïve, you have no idea how lovely you are. Irresistible. A dark madonna. Silky. Thick hair and wonderful gray-green cat eyes, and your goddamned body, so lithe and smooth. I don't want to share you at all. I don't want any other man to know you, or look at you or even talk to you. I want you cloistered, hidden and draped, like a Moslem woman. I want you exclusively and I want you to agree.

I can hear you laughing. You can't remotely understand, can you?

The letter went on for several more pages, becoming less and less coherent. I was in shock. He couldn't be serious, he couldn't really believe what he'd written. There was some mistake. But he wouldn't let me visit. And he wouldn't talk on the phone. He said we could talk at Thanksgiving.

By Thanksgiving he'd made up his mind. I made him explain, over and over, a dozen times, hoping that something might click and he'd change his mind.

First he talked about love in a rambling way; even he didn't know what he meant. I pressed him. *How could something so good be bad? Didn't he love me? Didn't he like my body?*

Of course, he said, but something bad happens. I don't like my feelings. When we're making love, I gloat and say to myself, *Look what I can make her do, look how much she wants me, look how I can make her beg*. I like to humiliate you. I love to watch you come—not because it gives you pleasure, but because I have the power to make you helpless.

Mona, he told me, that's not who I am—at least not the person I want to be. Not with you, anyway. I want us to stay friends. I want you in my life forever. I want us to be separate, thoughtful human beings. I care about you. Is that so strange?

I thought so. If he liked me so much, why couldn't we be lovers? Who cared what he was thinking? What he *did* was what mattered, and I thought what he did was fine. I was sure Matt was the right person. We matched each other. It was almost as if we'd been married for years. Just as my life was falling into place, becoming like the dream I'd imagined for years, Matt snatched it away. He made me feel wicked and unwanted. I was angry and hurt.

He kept saying that it wasn't love. That we weren't separate. That we were *too close*. That sex with me pushed him over the edge. That he lost himself.

I told Matt there was no such thing as *too close*. *Too close* was what I loved—that feeling of blending, merging, losing my edges. Melted wires.

No, he said, that's what I can't stand. It frightens me. So I change you into a warm hole, a fucking machine. I become a monster. I want to own you, to use you. He kept using the word *possess*. To me it was laughable. Careful, even, rational Matt. I told him no one could *possess* anyone.

That's not true, he insisted. With me, you become an object, a thing for me to exert power and control over. Don't you see how evil that is?

His words seemed melodramatic.

I tried to accept that Matt was telling me something real about himself—after all, why would he lie?—but it wasn't possible. I didn't understand. He seemed to be playing a cruel joke, and at my expense. Matt must have known how important he was; how he had allowed my life to begin; that I saw us as being like Mama and Papa. But no. He refused to admit that he was ruining my life. He was perverse and horrible. Why? My lovely Matt.

It was painful to see him, to know where he was, what he was doing, even to hear Grandpa saying his name. After one miserable year at Bryn Mawr, I transferred to the University of Toronto for a five-year degree in medical illustration. I thought that if I stayed away, Matt would change his mind. We'd never spent long stretches apart. I was sure he'd change.

15 TORONTO

Matt didn't change. I changed. Or perhaps I became more true to myself.

When I went to Toronto, I didn't understand how unusual it was that I'd read and studied Grandpa's books—Tyson and Stubbs and Casserius—that I could tell a Sobotta drawing from a Demarest without looking twice. Medical plates were part of my life. I'd been looking at anatomical renderings since I was six years old. I thought everyone knew them. It was hard to realize how much I'd absorbed, mostly because I'd never been taught formally, and had certainly never used what I knew. My drawings for Grandpa were no real test. His illustrator did the important plates for his book, and I did the mindless leftovers—the schematics, the charts, the line drawings. Drawers and notebooks were filled with my sketches, but they weren't for anyone in particular. Grandpa had seen them, and occasionally would suggest a subject or an approach, or would hand me a book he thought might be useful, but I'd never been tested in the field. How was I to know that the whole department in Toronto had been called in to see the work I sent with my application? And that Gluckman, who was chairman of the program and an old friend of Grandpa's, had called and talked to Grandpa for an hour about my career? I simply packed my pencils and left.

Grandpa didn't say much. He reminded me that Gluckman's reputation for being a tyrant was bluff. He could tell I was scared. But no one else could. My esoteric knowledge set me apart; my connections made the other students jealous. (On my first day, Gluckman appeared—a small, sandy-haired man with fierce eyes and a clipped mustache—greeted me by name, and came to my desk to ask about Grandpa; but then he ignored me, which was interpreted by the other students as approval, by me as neglect.)

I worked alone. Gross anatomy, applied art, embryology, pathology—for the first year I did nothing but work.

Matt wrote. I didn't write back. When he called, I was never in. He left messages at the reception desk of the medical school dormitory, where I had a room. Was I making friends? Did I like Gluckman? And last of all, was I coming home? Eventually? He said in his letters that we'd always be friends. He hadn't meant to drive me away, especially not away from Grandpa.

I still thought of Matt as my partner—just as Mama had been matched with Papa. When he called with his shabby offer of friendship, my stomach ached and I couldn't work. I didn't want to be teased with his voice, to be reminded that half of my life had ended.

"I'm fine," I told him the next time he called. "I'm friends with dead bodies. I have my cadavers."

When I talked like that, he left me alone.

What I said was true. By the end of the first semester I had stopped thinking of cadavers as dead people. They had become an independent class of objects, unrelated to human beings. They no longer represented a loss of something. I never wondered what they had done or who had loved them. For me, they had never lived. They were artifacts, subjects for study. They were as they were supposed to be.

The adjective *dead* didn't say anything new or useful. What interested me was the quality of the material at hand, the record of events embedded in flesh: enlarged spleens, battered livers, swollen ears. Cadavers were bristling with information, they had clear personalities and differences. They had had two lives, and in my view they were perhaps better known in the lab, the second time around.

Some people work with machines, others with ideas or formulas. My medium was body parts. In Toronto, I became a professional. Bladders and bones, canals and processes. I peered and manipulated and exposed their most telling arrangements. And then I fixed them in time on paper. Life became, for me, immortal. Who needed Matt? Who needed anyone?

Matt disagreed. He didn't want me himself, but he wanted more in my life than dead bodies. Had I been to Nathan Phillips Square? To the Royal Ontario Museum? I should be out and looking around.

His guilt was talking. I hated to hear it. Looking for what? I demanded. I know what I want. I want *you*. You're the missing part of my life. You're the only man I can love.

If I couldn't have Matt, at least I could work. It provided the only sufficient distraction.

A person needs more than work, he insisted.

Needs? I said. Am I allowed to have *needs*? What kind of needs? Matt didn't reply.

I'd always thought of physical needs as an indulgence. Part of Papa's elaborate idea of being human was the unspoken rule that needs were illegal. It wasn't chocolate or sex or naps that mattered, for these were innocent, neutral things, with no meaning in themselves. It was what needing these things betrayed: a lack of control, weakness of will. In our family, we never *needed* a nap, we *wanted* a nap. There was always choice, never compulsion. Acknowledging need was against the rules. Need was a sin.

Matt released me into the world—but not in the way that he'd intended. I abandoned the family ethic. I let myself go. I gave myself permission to acknowledge my body. If I couldn't have love, at least I could routinize need.

16 MISSIONARY POSITION

The first time was with a medical student, good looking and he knew it, but pale and bland, his personality submerged by too many years of study. We were sharing a cadaver and I shocked him by knowing so much. How could I know all this stuff, he asked, and still be, as he put it, "so nice." He might as well have spelled it out: *Where are your zits and your greasy hair? Your oxfords and long tweed skirt?*

For a while it was strictly studentish. We drank coffee together. I was pretty sure he wanted my notes; I was right, he did. But when he discovered I wasn't a medical student—that is, not competition—he saw me differently.

He asked me to dinner on a Saturday night, after a round of exams. I wore a dress, which he didn't expect, so he put on a jacket and took me to an expensive Italian restaurant in Yorkville—Toronto's equivalent of Georgetown—where we had a long, slow dinner. It reminded me too much of Italy, which I didn't like. Toward the end of dinner he pressed my hand and spoke his mind.

"Let's go back to my place."

We were sitting next to each other on a fake red leather banquette. He put his hand on my thigh. His other arm slid around my back and pulled me against him.

I opened my eyes wide.

"Afraid?" he said, rubbing my leg.

I lowered my eyes. The classic pose. How could he fall for it?

"What you need," he said, practicing his bedside manner, "is a good first experience." He looked serious. "You need to start on the right track."

I managed not to laugh. It was every man's fantasy. But why couldn't I take him at face value? I didn't know. I gave him a level look, and said, "Can *you* show me the right track?"

He smiled the same idiotic grin I was to see so many other times, with so many other men, when I popped an approximation of the same question. Of course he could help. He would be delighted! Another grin.

But I always refused a second go. "Just an introduction, remember?"

"But I—wasn't it—I mean—" he stammered, "I mean, didn't you—"

"Of course I did. You *know* I did."

"But that was only the beginning. Don't you want—I mean, don't we, can't we . . ."

I looked him directly in the eye. "You know I do. But how can I say yes to you, and then no to Robert and Raymond and James? This clearly isn't a matter of *love.*" I paused, knowing he wouldn't deny it. "So. How am I to conduct myself? I can't sleep with everyone, can I?"

He was stymied. They were all stymied. I was proposing to sleep with everyone, or no one, while in fact I was sleeping with everyone *once*: married professors, research assistants, students, lab technicians, even orderlies.

When Matt called to tell me his news—he was going to medical school, which was no surprise—and to quiz me about my life, I said, "Here's what I'm doing," and rattled off a list of first names. There was a long pause on the phone. He knew what I meant. After that, he stopped calling. He only wrote.

17 STEVE

One day at the beginning of my last year, a man came into the neuroanatomy lab. He moved around the room, looking over our shoulders. Finally, after wandering and looking for some time, he stood behind my chair and put a folded note on the table beside my papers. As he went out the door, I read the note: "Would you meet me for coffee after class? A professional matter. Steve Gilpin."

It was a lab class, with no set times. We usually stayed three or four hours. He must have known we were close to the end. I packed my tools and folded my work. I found him sitting on a bench outside the lab. I was sure he wanted charts or illustrations for an article he was writing. Toronto was full of American graduate students, avoiding the draft. He looked like a social-science type—bland and brushed and even handsome, in an anonymous way. We went to the coffee shop across the street from the university and took a booth. He ordered coffee and Danish. I was starved.

"Miss Emory," he said, "this is not the sort of medical illustration you usually do."

"Doesn't matter," I mumbled, between bites. I had done a little of everything with Grandpa: schematics, line drawings, even some experimental work mapping ultrasound. And I was used to making money.

He took out a smallish portfolio, eighteen by twenty-four. I pushed my dish to the end of the table. It was four in the afternoon, and the place was empty.

"Miss Emory," he said, "before I show you these, I want you to know that I think your work is exquisite. I've been to three universities, and your work is the best I've seen."

"Really?" I said. "Where've you been?" I was surprised and flattered. I wanted to know my competition. He told me he'd been to Hopkins, Texas, and UCLA, the high-tech anatomy places. He said my work was better than their shiny stuff. I liked that. He said my drawings were better than photographs.

He got me started. I went on about how I liked my drawings to look like sculpture, how I liked to use more than two colors. "It's more than aesthetics," I said, "it's a matter of accuracy." I waited.

"I couldn't agree more." His expression was serious.

"So," I said. "Let's see what you've got." I reached for the portfolio.

He put his hand over the tied string. "Miss Emory?" He caught my eye.

"You can call me Mona," I said.

"Mona," he said, and then paused. "Before you look, I want you to know we pay very well. And we respect your artistic sensibilities. Do you understand?"

"What's to understand? Just let me look at your prototypes." I was annoyed that he had gotten me to talk about my work, even if only superficially.

He opened the portfolio to a stack of rag boards, with tissue paper over the first drawing and between the subsequent pictures. I lifted the tissue. I felt my skin go clammy and then flush. It was all I could do to keep from fainting. It was pornography.

"Mona?"

"Just let me look through them all." I was struggling for

control, for a reaction I could present. I was shocked, angry, and also intrigued. I carefully lifted the tissue paper off each picture and re-stacked it on the other side of the portfolio. My body was heating up. That was the worst.

"I don't need money," I said. It wasn't true, but I needed something neutral to say. I didn't like taking money from Grandpa. He was already paying my tuition.

I imagined sending these pictures to Matt. Or ones like them. I imagined his face.

I looked up. A deep breath. "I can do better."

Steve Gilpin raised his eyebrows. "A challenge?"

I paused. "How many do you want?" My voice was quiet and low. I felt the vibration of my words in my throat, saw myself from a great distance, sitting at the table, fingering the tissue paper, looking at the pictures, and finally tilting my head, looking out of the sides of my eyes, and nodding at Steve.

18 MODELS

Steve hired actors and dancers as models. They had beautiful bodies and were terribly poor. He turned away the ones who were too thin. They wouldn't do. He wanted skin with a vitamin sheen.

It was like being a member of an exclusive club, where what was held in common was never discussed. Several of the models had worked for Steve before, which helped, but we never talked about what we did on the outside; no, we kept ourselves in a vacuum, as if we didn't exist outside this work we did together. We gathered on Friday mornings in an anonymous yellow brick building on Sherbourne Avenue. It was a part of town for people in flux, a neighborhood of cheap boardinghouses and residential hotels. I often stayed there with Steve on the weekends: an apartment with a bed in the living room, a carpeted platform with animal skins in the dining room, and, in the two bedrooms, backdrops, photographer's lamps, and a drafting table for me. It had the still air of closed rooms, rooms where many people had stayed. Steve didn't have to tell me who used the apartment during the week. A persistent alkaline odor floated throughout, the dry smell of need. And there were things in the bathroom: condoms, disinfectant, douching powders.

After working, Steve sent out for pizza or Chinese food,

and we ate ravenously. Steve paid. For the models, food was part of the deal. As a result, the kitchen trashcan was always full of greasy wrappings and the counters were ringed with coffee stains and littered with packets of sugar and soy sauce. There was no permanent place where anything belonged, no reason to be clean or neat, to wash things or put them away, except in the most expedient manner. It was domestic anarchy, which shocked me almost as much as what we were doing. It was unlike any place I'd ever been. It was not a home, but neither was it a workplace, an office or a lab, which, by constant occupancy, was eventually civilized. It was more like a bus station or terminal, always busy, always lit, always *there*, whether acknowledged or not, and now, for me, a place I had to know in myself, an unavoidable place I had to pass through in order to get wherever I was going.

We would arrive, Steve and I and however many models, usually three. They would undress and put on bathrobes and Steve would turn up the heat and before we started we'd sit around drinking coffee and discussing the Polaroids I'd taken the session before. It was a loose exchange. What worked, what didn't. They didn't mind. They were paid by the hour.

Steve was Canadian. He worked on commission for very rich clients. They were willing to pay, not only for the pictures they wanted, but for Steve's discretion as well. He was financing law school this way. He said it was safer than drugs. And more entertaining. My drawings were for an American collector. Steve described what his client wanted. Steve said he wanted explicit pictures, but didn't care about particular positions or anything like that. It wasn't *what* was portrayed that mattered, so much as *how* it was shown. His client wanted art, because art had feeling in it. He wanted tension, connection, struggle, desire. He wanted to see people in the grip of something, people being taken over by their bodies.

He wanted to see letting go, giving in, melting, and surrendering, as if sex were a battle and winning were losing.

After talking, we set up poses and I took more Polaroids and then sketched for an hour, sometimes longer. For the models, this was the whole job. For me, it was preliminary work, gearing up and getting ready. My real work was with Steve on the weekends. I got ideas then. We did things I'd never done before.

Steve rejected my first drawing. I was paid, of course, but it wasn't right. He tried to explain. He kept saying he wanted "the whole thing."

"Fake it," he said.

I looked puzzled.

He shook his head. "You don't know what I'm talking about, do you? You don't even know what 'the whole thing' is."

I didn't know.

"They glow," he said. "People in love. Like soft neon. You've got to draw love."

He suggested that I look at his prototypes again. Look hard, he told me. What do you see? The first time I'd been too shocked to look at anything but technique, the drafting, the scale, the color. I had distracted myself with aesthetic issues, and missed the real accomplishment of the pictures. Steve's patron wanted pictures of people in love, he wanted pictures of a profound connection, an electric current, an intense and palpable magnetism. Not just rutting. Not just humans in heat. It was hard. Impossible, perhaps. And yet he wanted dirty pictures.

Steve found new models, two dancers newly in love, but so broke they were almost too thin. They were young and fresh and trying to make it. And they were love distinct. The shiny eyes and locked gaze. The swollen parts. They must have been desperate.

Steve made them pose with another model, a man. Two men on one woman. It was cruel, but it made the girl light up. Her boyfriend's eyes became dark and glittered. He was determined to show he loved her best.

Can love be acted? Certainly, actors do it all the time. They learn how to do it. I could act too; I could pretend, in my drawings. I could draw it and twist it, just slightly, push past its truth, past its pure state, to something disturbing, explicit, and ultimately wrong to show. It was pornographic because it was private. A kind of invasion. I did that, again and again, four series, sixteen pictures. I drew my parents.

Love looks like this. The lips swell, the eyes are bright and slightly closed, the pupils large and wet. Feathery skin, the air around the body faintly blue, and the body itself glowing, as if from within, with a pale fluorescent flush. All openings are swollen, shining, taut, with a slightly metallic sheen, everything pushed out, glossy, expanded, reaching. Love art. But not love.

Behind each picture, each close view, I drew circles of flesh, long limbs, sconces and swags of organs and members, in repeating patterns and borders, like Edwardian wallpaper.

Their bodies were beautiful.

Steve kept one room for us. A double bed and two windows, looking up into a huge old maple tree, its leaves flaming with fall color. What we did there was extremely effective, technically perfect, and I liked having my body worked over. I liked not having to pretend that anything else was going on. But that was all it was, only my body. No light. I couldn't produce the feelings. Not the part where everything glows and floats. It was never the way I'd felt with Matt.

The red leaves fell from the tree. Winter set in. Without

telling Steve, I photographed each of the drawings I made and sent them to Matt for Valentine's Day. Under each photograph I wrote this quotation from Rilke: *"Why are we not set in the midst of what is mysteriously ours?"*

I wanted Matt to tell me why.

19 COPROLINS

I didn't expect such a literal answer.

Matt send Mama's letters. They came in March. The letters Noel had given me. From that day on, after the letters arrived, the events of my life in Toronto followed one another inevitably, like dominoes falling. Leaving wasn't part of a plan. It simply happened.

"He won't leave me alone," Mama wrote. *"He's after my smell. He wants the smell of a woman in heat. Even worse,"* she wrote, *"I can't hold out. After he does certain things, I'm possessed,"* she wrote. *"I'm lost. He knows I'm ready. He says he can smell it. Coprolins, he calls it. Fatty acids. The human pheromone. He sniffs and smiles. He says he has just what I want."*

Love, I kept thinking. What about love? I pored over the letters, looking for some mention of love. But Mama never wrote about love. Her letters didn't use the word once. They were about what he did; what he made her do; and about what, in the end, she was feeling and wanting to do. Was that love? That way of being together? If so, it wasn't what I'd imagined. It was shocking.

I thought it was the letters that made me sick. It started with what I thought was flu—an upset stomach for a week, and then for a second week. It wasn't enough to keep me in bed, but I'd never felt this bad before. I was sure I was sick from knowing. It finally occurred to me that I might have an ulcer, so I went to a doctor at Student Health, who took blood and urine and sent me back to the dorm. He would call, he said, and when he did, it was to tell me to come in for a series of injections of penicillin. I had gonorrhea.

I felt unclean. I told myself it could be rinsed away, diluted with incessant baths and douching. But it wasn't something on the outside, to be washed away, it was inside. My entire self felt rank and polluted. And then it became more than pollution. I had been invaded, overrun. It had been encroaching for a long time, creeping up; without my knowledge, I had been under siege, and now it was entrenched in me. I was infested and being ravaged. There were cells dividing and attacking, multiplying and spreading their purulent evil all through my body. I was an outpost of the enemy. My body had betrayed me. My body had always been strong, resisting attack, a partner in my enterprises. My body had always obeyed. But now my body was possessed and was no longer mine. My body would produce nothing valuable. It would make nothing. I was useless, spoiled, and becoming evil.

Within three weeks my physical symptoms were gone, but not the effects of the letters. They told more than I wanted to know: that Mama hadn't been in charge of her body; that her feelings and thoughts had been at odds. The repulsive idea that Papa was studying how she smelled hadn't changed her behavior; she had still given in. They were physically wrapped. He had had her in thrall.

What was Matt trying to tell me? That love wasn't simple? That romance was a myth of my own creation? Or was he trying to say something about me? About us? About what we had done together and what I was doing now, in Toronto? Was he telling me that I couldn't control my body?

It seemed fitting. I was being punished. Matt had answered my question. This was what was mysteriously mine. This.

It was spring. The buds were swelling on the red maple tree outside the apartment window on Sherbourne Avenue. The doctor at Student Health had suggested I tell my partners. I was pale and thin. It was my senior year, and I had my thesis to finish. I decided to stop drawing for Steve. I would finish my work for school, take the summer off, and look for a real job in the fall.

When I told Steve I wouldn't do a new series, and that furthermore he should see a doctor, he said he had medication already—that he, in fact, was the source of my problem. He had "forgotten" to tell me. He became suddenly busy, too busy to answer my calls, to have dinner or spend weekends together, as we used to do. He was working, he said. He dropped me flat. I was strictly business.

And then Julie's wedding invitation came—a thick buff envelope full of engraved enclosures and tissue paper. On the bottom of the invitation she had written a short note, still in her schoolgirl hand, with circles over the *i*'s and exclamation points: "At last! It's the real thing! We're moving to California. Kisses, J." I ran my finger over the raised printing of her name and burst into tears. Everyone was leaving or doing something real and serious. And what was I doing?

I called Grandpa, still in tears. I told him I'd been sick and working too hard and my life seemed to be falling apart. My friends were leaving, Julie was getting married, school was finishing, and what was I doing in Toronto, anyway, sick with the clap and drawing dirty pictures? I didn't explain myself further, or expect him to understand, I just wept and raged, and Grandpa listened and asked no questions. That was his way. It always had been.

The next week he wrote me a letter. His illustrator was retiring. She was seventy-five and had done half of the plates for his book. She had declared that halfway was her stopping place. She wanted to sit on her dock in Wisconsin. She had grandchildren there and fish to catch. She knew I was graduating. She told Grandpa to call me home.

It was like him to make it seem her idea. I knew it was his. He suggested coming home for the summer. There was plenty of room, he said. Piero was away for the summer and would be starting college in the fall. Prima had just been awarded her Ph.D. and was teaching in St. Louis. She rarely came home. The house was empty. We could rattle around together. "Come on home," he wrote, "just to see." *To see what?* I wondered. To see if I'd misbehave at home? To see if I was good enough? I *was* good enough. I knew the job was mine for the asking.

20 REMEDIAL AGENTS

I came back to Washington in June, settled into the house, and started working for Grandpa and eventually for other doctors at the medical school. I felt as if I'd never left, as if what I'd done in Toronto had actually happened here, in my old rooms, in my parents' rooms, in this house in Washington—as if, all along, I'd been living in and breathing that same old atmosphere. Toronto itself became a dream. This felt real. It all had actually happened here.

Initially, I started swimming as a way of using my body alone. And as a kind of cleansing. I was exhausted and out of shape. After a month of swimming every day in the Georgetown University pool, my muscles lengthened and every part of me flowed together in smooth, continuous, complex curves. Swimming gave me a feeling of completeness and overview. In the water, nothing mattered, I didn't live anywhere, not in Toronto or Washington or anywhere. As I swam back and forth, up and down, over and over, I became unconscious of moving my arms and legs and lost the feeling of having a body. I swam in a self-hypnotic trance, my mind blank and remote, my arms mechanically stroking the blue stripe of water. After moving around in a swimming pool, my self dissolved, the pressure was off, and I felt nothing at all.

Matt had been in medical school. He came back to Washington the year after I did, to start a residency in psychiatry at George Washington University Medical School. When Grandpa told him about my swimming, he laughed and said, Mona is married to a body of water.

I imagined a blue rectangle standing next to me at a church altar, flat and translucent, the way pools appear from airplanes.

Matt said I wasn't running away, I was swimming away.

I said it was better than the missionary position.

He laughed a little nervously. I watched his face go pale.

Why don't you join a team? he suggested.

It was a wonderful reversal.

I told him I didn't care about improving my crawl or joining a masters' team. I told him I swam for that soft endorphin high, that feeling of absence, nothing more.

Matt said I was addicted.

So what? I said. You're addicted to weird people. I was alarmed that he'd chosen psychiatry. It seemed so passive. As if he were waiting for something. I told him so. He gave me a look. Had I seen some shred of the truth? I persisted. "Matt. What happened?"

He smiled a sweet, archaic smile that made his bony face look boyish and silly.

"Well?" I said.

"We've been through that."

"Let's go through it again."

"It won't make any difference."

"You read those letters," I said. "What did you think?"

He wouldn't answer.

"You think I'm just like Mama—isn't that right?"

He never denied it. He never said anything, which infuriated me. When he refused to talk, as he did so often, I used to get the smell of myself on my fingers, and hold them in front of his nose. "You used to like this smell," I said. "You said so in Venice. Don't you remember?"

More silence from Matt.

"If I'm like Mama, then you're like Papa. Isn't that so? Is that what scares you? That we might be like them?" I was willing to do almost anything to get a reaction. I was outraged. It was Matt who had made me act like Mama. It was his fault. I wanted to spread the pain. That was when I first got home. But even then, when I made things hard for him, he'd simply get up and leave the room. I never once saw his eyes light up in the old way.

Most of the time I wanted him to explain. I returned to the subject again and again, obsessed with how he conducted his life. All our conversations ended with my not understanding, and with his silence. The more I pressed, the more veiled and remote he became. So I kept on swimming. And the Bishops came.

I'd been home two years. It was a Saturday, in the fall. I was at the lab, but Grandpa was visiting Matt when they came, and he described their arrival at dinner that night. Matt was clipping back the clematis vine on his front porch. Both he and Grandpa heard a rustling behind the front privet hedge, and then the sound of liquid flowing. They thought it was Sheeba, the dog next door, until they heard voices and peeked through the hedge.

"You fucker! Where'sa tissue?"

"No more tissue."

"Shit on you."

"Use your skirt."

No response.

"Use your *under*skirt."

"I done used it, asshole!"

"Ain't my fault we got no tissue."

"Is so. You tooks it all."

"Fuck I did."

Matt peered through the hedge and saw two obscenely fat and ragged people—a man and a woman. The woman's face was moon-shaped and doughy, a small nose and rosebud lips, a child's features gone pinched and suspicious. *Sly* was the word that Grandpa used. The man looked like a pig—his whole face pointing forward toward a gross, thick nose with huge black pores. Tiny eyes squinted out from folds of fat. He raised his head and sniffed.

"You got somethin', you whore, I can tell. I can smell somethin', so give it here." He snatched at the woman. She pulled away, but he grabbed her with one arm and started pulling up layers of skirt with the other.

"You pile of rags, give it here!" He worked himself under her skirts. She swatted at him with the thick fingers of her open hands.

"Aha. Aha!" The man emerged, waggling his index finger like a fat worm in front of her eyes. "You bitch, don'tcha know better'n to hold out on your man?" He held up a cellophane-wrapped rectangle of yellow cheese. "I smelt it. I did. I knows how you smells. There were something fresh, I knowed there was, I gots a good smeller." He tapped his nose and leered into her face. "Don'tcha never hold out on me, you bitch. Don'tcha keep *nothin'* back, you hear me?"

She glared at him, and as he turned to open the cheese, she raised her hand and swung it back behind her shoulder like a tennis racket and gave him an enormous wallop, knocking him off his feet and onto the pavement. The cheese flew out of his hand and onto the grass next to the hedge.

"Now look what you done, you spoilt it for both us. Look here, you flang it right where we pissed. Asshole."

"Just wipe it, that's all, it be fine."

He picked up the cheese and threw it at her. "You wipe it, you fat pile of rags. You spoilt it, you wipe it." He sneered and adjusted himself between his legs and glinted his pig eyes at her.

They moved closer to the thick privet hedge. Matt and Grandpa couldn't see, but they heard grunts and swearing and finally silence.

Matt and Grandpa were still staring at each other when the two huge ragged figures turned in the walk and marched up the steps to Matt's front porch.

"We come home." The man was addressing Matt.

The woman took a step forward. "This be our house. We used to live here and—"

"—we wanna come back."

"We helped with the Misses." She looked at Matt expectantly.

21 DEVOTED TO CELIBACY

That was the beginning. Things were never the same after Tildy and Hiram Bishop made their claim. Matt let them in. Grandpa didn't say a word, but when Lilla heard about it, she had a fit. She remembered the Bishops. She said they'd worked at Matt's house—years before, when Matt was little—but that when Matt's father had found out they'd been in a mental institution, he'd sent them packing. As Lilla had said, "Crazy folks is no kind of help to poor Miz Louise."

Matt's father had retired from his lobbying job on the Hill and moved back to Georgia. His mother had died. Matt could do as he pleased with the house. Shortly after the Bishops came, he replaced the antique furniture with vinyl sofas and plastic chairs and covered the oak parquet floors with brown and white squares of linoleum tile. It looked like a public clinic. I wouldn't go in; it was too painful. He was getting ready. All across the country, patients from public mental institutions were being released into the community. Even before he finished his residency, Matt had opened a halfway house.

He started talking about Marcie Horner. We all knew her. Her family had lived in Georgetown for years, back when it was still a slum. She still lived in the tiny, falling-down frame house on Volta Place, where she had taken care of her retarded older brother. It was a shame, people said, and an eyesore too. The yard was overgrown and filled with trash. There were rats, they said. There had been talk of having the house condemned. Matt wondered if Marcie would qualify for his house. He wasn't sure. She wasn't the usual type of street person—pushing an empty baby carriage or a shopping cart full of old clothes. She had a new twist. She pushed an empty wheelchair, and lied about why. Everyone knew the real reason, because they'd known her before, when Gabe was alive. But no one wanted to risk a scene. Who knew what she'd do? She might fall apart, right there on the street. Then what?

Matt had been watching Marcie for months. "She's different," he said. "She took care of Gabe as well as herself. Surely this wheelchair-pushing is a temporary thing." He waited. Six months. A year. She was still pushing. Something had to be done. He wanted her version of the story. All he knew was neighborhood gossip, the facts that become explanations but never really are: "Oh, she's just like that. You know Marcie. Been like that since Gabe died." A shrug. That was enough for most people. But not for Matt.

Matt didn't categorize people. To him, labels were irrelevant. "We're all in the same boat," he said. "We're human beings. Being alive is all that counts. Getting through each day. Brains, looks, money, choices, they aren't earned, having those things is a matter of luck."

Matt had become a behaviorist and a genetics man. He didn't believe people could or should be "fixed." They could be retrained, at best. He thought everything was set from birth. The double-helix approach to destiny. Our only choice was our attitude. His attitude was to cherish life. Any life.

Marcie could cope; she'd shown that she could. Matt said that was what bothered him. One summer evening he came over to sit in the garden. He'd finally decided. "It's her eyes," he said. "You've seen her eyes—they're blank and blue and you can't see in—as if the light has gone out inside." Nothing else about her had fallen apart. "She's held together by habit," he said. "She can't give up the habit of wheeling that chair around to the Safeway and to the Riggs Bank and to Montrose Park. She refuses to put her groceries in the seat where Gabe used to sit. She puts them on the footrest, where Gabe used to hold them in with his knees. She has an awful time, of course, and the groceries fall constantly. That's how I met her. I walked out of the Georgetown Safeway one day to find her bent over a spilled grocery bag, her carton of milk dripping a messy puddle on the stained sidewalk, and oranges rolling in every direction. I stopped and helped. I loved that she didn't explain, and that after I'd picked up her oranges, she offered me one."

Matt looked up at me. "I asked her to join the house," he said. "I told her I needed some help."

Matt had become a careful person. He thought for a long stretch before he said anything—his silences were more pronounced than whatever he said—and he was painfully careful to say what he meant, as if words themselves could cause permanent damage. He rarely made a promise of any kind. He said he didn't believe in them. Everything he said was considered, separately and carefully and individually. He enunciated precisely and spoke slowly and softly, as if each word weighed a pound and were being doled out from a limited supply.

In the end, what persuaded me to accept Matt's new self was that he still made fudge. When I passed his house on the way to the lab, I would smell it cooking. If he'd stopped making fudge, I would've been suspicious. But no, every week, out came the Baker's chocolate and the sweet butter and the extra-fine sugar and his black-bottomed fudge pot and he boiled and stirred, and to my surprise and, yes, I admit it, my disappointment, the fudge was perfect every time. His people loved it, just as I had. Matt said he'd finally learned the trick to keeping it smooth—a glossy pool on the ironstone plate, velvety, like baby food, and outrageously sweet. He'd learned to wait, he said; fudge was a maturity test. It was a matter of patience.

At first I was angry. I wished he'd gotten it perfect for *me*, instead of for them. I couldn't understand why he didn't have a private practice, why he didn't see patients and run an office, or at least a clinic, or even associate himself with one of the hospitals.

"Remember your Tyson," Matt said. "He wasn't just an anatomist. He worked at Bedlam. He was the first to offer post-institutional care. It's a noble tradition."

I told him what he could do with his Tyson.

I asked him if he really wanted to live his life with a bunch of ambulatory schizophrenics, and he said they didn't bother him, they only bothered me. He had time for the writing he wanted to start, and welfare paid his expenses. It was a perfect arrangement. They needed each other.

"It's a horrible arrangement," I said. "You could help people who want to change, people who—"

"People who want to change do it themselves. They find a way. But some people can't. They alter the world instead of themselves. I find them interesting."

I was angry. "You're choosing to live with permanent adolescents. All because you never rebelled yourself!"

He was amused when I went on like this. He called it "Mona's parlor analysis." He would never talk about personal things, about our life before.

Tyson was Grandpa's hero, and now had become Matt's model as well. I remembered reading that while Tyson was working, he had "devoted himself to celibacy." Devoted. I liked the word. I liked the idea. Enough was enough. In my own way, I could be like Tyson, too. I gave up on Matt, on the idea of anyone in my life. I would preempt disappointment. I would get more done.

I stopped expecting to enjoy myself. All I wanted was to fit in the world like everyone else, with a job and errands, the regular things. I wanted to join the ranks of everyday people who wake up each morning, get dressed, go to work, eat lunch, and then watch the day slide to its close. I wanted the necessity of a job. There was comfort in it. Order and pattern seemed attractive. Each day was planned, and held no surprises. Work for five days, rest for the other two. On Sundays, after swimming, I took walks or puttered in the garden, and reviewed my work for the coming week. Sunday evenings, Matt came for dinner. My life became a series of reassuring routines and continued, undisturbed, as glassy and smooth as a vacant swimming pool.

PART II

I should like to go back once more to the instinctual life of obsessional neurotics and add one more remark upon it. It turned out that our patient, besides all his other characteristics, was a renifleur. *By his own account, when he was a child he had recognized everyone by their smell, like a dog; and even when he was grown up he was more susceptible to sensations of smell than most people. I have met with the same characteristic in other neurotics, both in hysterical and obsessional patients, and I have come to recognize that a tendency to taking pleasure in smell, which has become extinct since childhood, may play a part in the genesis of neurosis. And here I should like to raise the general question whether the atrophy of the sense of smell (which was an inevitable result of man's assumption of an erect posture) and the consequent organic repression of his pleasure in smell may not have had a considerable share in the origin of his susceptibility to nervous disease. This would afford us some explanation of why, with the advance of civilization, it is precisely the sexual life that must fall a victim to repression. For we have long known the intimate connection in the animal organization between the sexual instinct and the function of the olfactory organ.*

—Sigmund Freud, *The Collected Papers of Sigmund Freud*, vol. III, ed. Ernest Jones, trans. Alix and James Strachey

22 GRANDPA'S BOOK

On my way downstairs, I glanced out the landing window and saw a tall man with dark straight hair coming out of the house next door. Grandpa was walking along the sidewalk, and when the two men met, each stopped to let the other go first. I saw Grandpa step back in surprise, and then quickly move forward, his arm extended to shake hands.

I watched the two men talking. Grandpa pointed in the direction of the university, and the man with dark hair tilted his head and fingered his open collar with a questioning look. Grandpa shrugged. The man signaled "Wait a minute," and strode back up the steps of the house. A moment later he reappeared with a tie dangling around his neck, and a tweed coat slung over his shoulder.

Right then, I knew it was Charles. The house next door had been occupied for years by a retired navy admiral and his blue-haired, corseted wife. We'd never really gotten to know them. Grandpa had said they were moving to Florida, but I hadn't realized they'd only been renting the house. Charles was back.

I watched the two men set off together down the street, talking and glancing at one another, Grandpa occasionally raising his stick to point out this or that, and Charles slipping his tie into a knot. They were going to the party for Grandpa's book.

I wore my navy dress and Mama's pearls; Grandpa was dressed in what Lilla called his funeral suit—charcoal-gray pinstripes and a matching vest—with his watch chain draped across his belly. Collared and starched and swinging his cane, he looked more like a riverboat gambler than like Gabriel Emory, Professor Emeritus, author of a distinguished anatomy text. His standard garb was a worn jacket, shiny pants, and pipe ashes dribbling over his tie.

This wasn't the usual university party, held in a cavernous cinder-block room. Instead, we gathered at the house of the dean of the medical school: clipped yew in front of leaded windows; worn Oriental rugs; the smell of paste wax on parquet floors. Instead of jug wine and processed cheese, tail-coated waiters circulated with trays of champagne and hot hors d'oeuvres. It was quite an event. There were lots of people.

My throat felt tight, but I didn't know why. To keep myself busy, I looked at the art. On the wall above the dean's desk was a hand-tinted engraving of Healy Hall, the oldest building on campus, and a series of eighteenth-century drawings of surgical instruments, beautifully matted and framed. On the desk itself, an original edition of Vesalius was open to a view of the skeleton, elegantly posed over its open grave. Dean Chasen was brave to leave it out; our copy was kept under lock and key. I turned the pages.

Grandpa came up behind me and touched my arm. "Olfactoria from Dean Chasen," he said, handing me a florist's box. It was a corsage of red rosebuds. He was wearing a boutonniere. Then he said, "And now a surprise." I saw a tall man with a worn-looking face and dark hair swept off his forehead. So this was Charles. He put out his hand and said

"Pomona." He smelled foreign. No one had called me Pomona in years.

"You don't remember?"

I had decided not to. "I'm sorry," I said. I studied his face. He had deep parentheses around his mouth, and furrows in his forehead. How old was he? Prima's age. He was thirty-two. He looked older.

"Charles." He paused, then added, "Sylvester."

I was still making my face look blank.

"I lived next door? Our parents worked together sometimes—your mother and my father?"

"Of course," I said. "I'm terribly sorry. It's been—"

"I know. A long time."

I stared at his shoes, smooth brown loafers. They looked very soft. Did he really believe I couldn't remember? Our games, our club, our endless summers. The curtains billowing. All of us walking to Montrose Park over the herringbone pattern of the brick sidewalk with Grandpa. The mock orange blooming, and the flowering crab with its pink smell. Papa coming home for lunch. Their open window and the strange sounds, gasps and sighs, falling into the garden. Prima going to boarding school. Charles leaving. My retreat to the lab with Matt and Grandpa.

"So," I said, "did you continue the family chocolate business?"

"They want a Washington office. It's required these days. And I have other work as well." He caught my eye. "It feels odd to be back. Very nostalgic."

I looked at his silk paisley tie and the fine, tight weave of his shirt. He had a well-bred sheen about him. I looked around the room, at people busy talking and eating, and then back to his face. I waved my hand at the crowd.

"After years in the lab, this feels unreal. I prefer being a name in small print in Grandpa's book."

Charles shrugged and opened his hands. I was waiting for him to ask about Prima. We watched the crowd. A waiter came and offered hot pastries. Charles took one, and then looked up with a smile. "Well, then, tell me about Prima. And Piero, too. I'm very sorry about your parents. I should have written."

"That was years ago. You were a child."

"So were you. What a shock. And a big change . . ."

"I guess it was." I wiped my fingers on my napkin. "Prima lives in St. Louis. She just got tenure. Pathology. Piero's here somewhere." I gestured to the room. "He's in medical school."

Behind Charles, I saw Grandpa across the room, heading our way with the sales representative from Williams and Wilkins. When they arrived, I introduced Charles and excused myself.

He was right, of course. Things had changed when they died. But not the way he thought.

23 HIDDEN STRUCTURES

My drawings looked real. They weren't like pictures of plastic models, but they weren't photo-realism either. Most medical texts have photographs paired with schematic drawings, the details labeled on each one. You have to keep looking back and forth, because neither picture presents the truth. My illustrations were different. They presented an intermediate image, somewhere between the unreadable photograph and the unrealistic, cleaned-up view. I showed structure without destroying form. It was a balancing act, and I was good at it. My pictures weren't always easy to read; they showed layers of fat, blood everywhere, viscera flopping, the mesentery stringing and tenting itself all over. But my images were true, and in the end, that was a bigger help. Grandpa said so. Everyone did.

I knew how to show the way things really looked, because Grandpa had taught me the difference between dissection and surgery. That was the clue, knowing how to take things apart, how to be delicate in a situation that was inherently indelicate. Grandpa had taught me to slide inside a body, to live in flesh and organs. After six hours of staring and poking and teasing parts apart with a tiny needle, man-made things looked gross and imprecise. Nothing compared with the human body.

I used to feel hurt when people didn't understand, when they would sniff and squeeze their faces shut, saying, *How could you?* I could feel their disgust when they started talking about *smelly flesh, messy flesh*.

The body's not messy, I wanted to tell them; the body is beautiful. It's the most articulate thing you have. Your *mind* is what's messy—your words and thoughts and mixed-up feelings. The body is exquisite and productive and useful. The body has meaning.

Of course, I never said anything, but it bothered me that no one understood how I felt. Except Grandpa. And maybe Matt.

The body could never be understood completely by cutting and exposing this or that muscle or organ. The body was not designed to be inspected that way. You had to unwrap it like a precious package, the way Vesalius did. In one of Grandpa's books, the illustrator, Bidloo, showed the reality of dissection: the slab with the body on it, the different knives, the hook for holding up the cadaver, the channels for draining blood, the wedges and chisels and saws. He showed not only the body and its structures, but his tools and techniques as well. There was no question that the body on the table was dead and being dismantled.

In my drawings, I tried for the same effect, to remind the viewer that the inspection process was imperfect and could never tell all. I wanted to show what happened when the body was invaded by man. I was realistic but still respectful. And I told the truth: our invasion created disorder; it wasn't intrinsic.

Once, when I was in high school, Julie had come over in a fit of giggles. She'd been at her religion class. She only went to keep peace at home, and to avoid being sent to a Catholic school; she laughed at everything they said.

She drew herself up tall, made a pompous face, and began

to recite: "The bodee"—she dragged out the word—"the bodeee is a temple. It is something to *worship*, to treat with *reverence* and *spiritual respect*." We laughed and she pranced around the room, repeating again and again, "Here is my *bodee*, here is my *temple*—are there any *worshipers*?" I laughed too, but in an odd way, I understood what her teachers were saying. I felt the same. The body was a miracle; it demanded respect. It was as close as we'd ever come to magic.

Living people, on the other hand, were mostly mysteries. Mama and Papa. Matt. Noel. Even Grandpa. They were much harder to understand. I didn't have an equivalent way of making such a close inspection. There was no way to dissect the self. Other clues and techniques were needed, but I didn't know them.

Matt said the only way was time. He said people became known—to themselves and to others—by logging in hours and years together; by raising children, sorting laundry and raking leaves; by being together as time slipped by. And how did I spend the bulk of my time? With cadavers at the anatomy lab.

When the book party was over, I walked home with Grandpa and Charles. How strange it felt, Charles walking beside me, reminding me of that old time and what we once had been—open and free for adventure. I sensed that he was still that way, while the rest of us were terribly different. He was acting as if we could begin again, just like that, where we'd left off twenty years before. Couldn't he see that we weren't the same? That we were all changed? Prima lived in St. Louis and rarely came home. Matt lived in his halfway house. Grandpa was old and about to retire. And I had my work. We all had forgotten our unfinished games.

We kicked our way through leaf piles and across a citron sea of ginkgo leaves. The air was yellow and smelled of decay. I thought about the coming of winter, how I liked the world stripped down to bark and rock, so that hidden structures revealed themselves: the understory of laurels, tangled nests, fallen trees. I liked to see the relations of things. I preferred the world known.

I remembered Charles and his golden box, and how, long after he'd left, we'd still talked about what might be inside. I no longer cared. I hadn't cared for a very long time.

24 THE BLACK POOL

In Washington, it's often possible to spend Thanksgiving in shirtsleeves, walking along the canal, watching the river flash through bare trees. But the year that Grandpa's book was published, the same year that Charles came back, winter came early. One Sunday morning in early November, Clipper asked me to gather the last tomatoes, and as I wrapped them in newspaper to ripen on the pantry shelf, my hands smelled viny and green. Clipper spent the day putting the garden to bed: perennial borders layered with hay, vegetable beds forked over with fresh manure from the Rock Creek stables. It seemed early to shut things down. Wasn't he rushing the season? But no, Clipper was right. Two days later, a hard frost blackened the marigolds and curled the chrysanthemums to brown husks.

"In November?" I said. "You're building a pool?"

Charles shrugged. "I should get a good price."

As if the price mattered. I looked at him with disbelief. He had the space, it wasn't that, or even the weather, really. It was the outrage of building a pool—slam, bang—like that. In our family we would have spent a year discussing the pros and cons, and then another six months arguing about design; and then we'd get bored. It would never happen. Yes, we would say, a good idea in theory, but so much trouble and work, just for swimming. But not Charles. He still had the same relentless energy flooding out in different directions. There was his chocolate office, a proposal he was writing for the Smithsonian, and now a swimming pool.

"What color?" I asked.

"Black," he said, "like a New England pond. I love ponds. Limnology."

"Who?"

"The study of ponds. Of fresh water, really." He ran his fingers through his hair.

We were standing outside; the light was almost gone. I felt I should ask him in for supper, but it was Lilla's day off, which meant canned soup and grilled cheese sandwiches. I'd never bothered to learn cooking. Lilla organized everything. There were different menus for each season, chosen by Papa, long ago, so it never occurred to me to go to the grocery store and stand over an array of packaged meats glowing under pink lights and wonder what to make for dinner. It had all been arranged. The physical world of menus and meals, what seeds to plant, what colors to paint the walls or upholster the chairs—all those things had been Papa's domain, and his influence still reigned in the house. I never thought of domestic things.

I looked over at Charles. He probably cares what he eats, I thought. I'll bet he even likes to cook. How did he seem to make things happen all the time? How did he seem to know what he wanted? While he went on about swimming pools and Washington summers, I shifted my feet and tried to remember why we hadn't built a pool long before.

"Let's go out to dinner," he said.

"Grandpa's alone."

"Ask him along."

I shrugged and stamped my feet. "He never eats out."

"I'll ask anyway." Charles strode through the gate and up the steps, and was back outside before I had reached the portico.

"He says he's happy with Tyson. Is that something to eat?"

"No." I smiled. "It's one of his books. *The Anatomy of a Pygmie.*"

"You know it too?"

"Sure. Tyson is Grandpa's hero. He was the first scientist to show the link between man and the animal kingdom. He studied the anatomy of a chimpanzee." I paused. "I was raised with Grandpa's books. Hunter's *Gravid Uterus* was my Mother Goose."

Charles took my arm. "It's cold," he said, steering me down the street. "Come tell me about the *Gravid Uterus*. The Georgetown Grill has a fireplace."

"No," I said, unhooking my arm. "Another time."

Charles followed me back to the steps and watched me go in. He knew I wanted to go.

Everyone had something to do. Piero was on clinical rotations and left the house before it was light, and spent every other night and weekend at the hospital. When I did see him, he sounded discouraged. The medical service—with diabetes, ulcers, and heart attacks—made him impatient. He hadn't found what he wanted yet. I wasn't worried. It was clear to me that he'd end up a surgeon. He chaffed at interim measures. He liked physical problems with concrete solutions. He was a fixer. He would become a biomechanic.

Grandpa went every day to his office at the university to answer his mail and sort his papers. Although he had officially retired when the book was published, he kept his office for writing. After lunch in the faculty dining room, he strolled home and spent the afternoon browsing in his books, and reading papers colleagues had sent. He seemed preoccupied and remote. We passed each other in silence, acknowledging one another only enough to avoid contact, as if not speaking made us invisible and permitted us to ignore the fact that we were no longer working together.

Charles could've had a chauffeur and a private car, but instead he took the bus downtown. One day, when we met on the sidewalk, he said in that blithe way of his, "Come on, walk me to the bus." I did, and somehow we started a habit: everyday we walked together to Wisconsin Avenue, where he got on the 30 bus. He assumed I was walking to work, and I assumed he was heading downtown to his chocolate office. But I didn't ask. I suppose I was jealous. He had a job. Several jobs. Mine was finished.

When I came home from Toronto, I hadn't expected to love my work. I'd simply wanted to fill each day, get through each week, January to February, February to March. But Grandpa's book became more than a job, even more than vocation. It became my life. Weeks used to pass—*whoosh*—like a bloom of flame, without my noticing. Five years went by in a flash. I had a calling.

But my calling seemed to end with the book. It didn't matter that I'd been offered jobs at Hopkins and NIH. I couldn't muster the interest. I felt too tired to start something new. There were leftover jobs I could do at the lab, if I chose to do them. I would wait until spring. Both Hopkins and NIH said they would wait. I didn't care.

Quite suddenly, all I had was time. I noticed aspects of the world I'd never seen before. I noticed how every day was different. I noticed the weather and what people were wearing and how they arranged their faces to start their days. I did things I'd never had time for before: I went to the library, I walked Charles to the bus. I took walks around Georgetown. I did errands for Lilla. I took the long route everywhere—to the pool, to the lab—and spent hours looking at houses. It wasn't just their Georgetown charm, the shapes and details and packed-togetherness. It was something else. I started to sketch them.

When I was drawing houses, I enjoyed thinking how different they were, but I couldn't imagine choosing one, I couldn't imagine saying, *Yes, I want this one, with painted brick and tiny colonial rooms. Or that one, with huge windows and wrought-iron balconies.*

I would stop to look at a brick wall. Who lived behind that wall? What did they do and what did they own? What made them happy? In every house, people were living the lives they had chosen. My only real choice was my work. That was where I'd lived for the past five years. How had that happened?

25 CADAVERS

It was a frozen January day, a day muffled by low gray clouds and the smell of snow. Georgetown was empty and still, immobilized by cold, and there were no sounds, not even crows. I was walking with Charles.

"Your family business is death," he announced in that mild-mannered way he had.

"We describe the body. That's very different."

"I see," he said. Meaning he didn't.

We stopped at Wisconsin Avenue to wait for the light. As we started to cross, he took my arm and tucked it under his. It felt strange to be attached. I looked into his face. What did I know about him? Nothing. He was a stranger who had somehow adopted the privileges of a long-standing family friend. I wasn't sure I liked that. I wasn't sure what I felt about Charles. When we'd crossed the street, I detached my arm. "I don't pretend to know about why, but I do know this: we preempt death. And without death, life has no meaning."

"Are you speaking for yourself," he said, "or for the family?"

"For myself. Now, anyway." I stopped for a moment and looked up at him. The words rushed out. "Don't you see—I was grateful for my work, for something engrossing to think about, a demanding job that took my time and my skill. It was more than a job. It was a way to fit in, a niche designed exactly for me. I loved it. I was good at it. And it was useful. I had found my place. Everything was settled."

I stopped to stare into a store window. The display was of dozens of clocks—for the new year, I supposed.

"I chose my work. I couldn't wait to get up in the morning, don't you see, I was happy, that's it, I was . . ."

Did Grandpa know that he'd rescued me, way back then, when he first took me to the lab? He must have known, but he never talked about it. Grandpa never talked about anything. That wasn't his way of helping. One thing led to another and neither of us thought to ask why or how it got started; we never examined our lives for meanings. It wasn't a family habit. All our thinking was about work. No one had ever asked, *Mona, why are you taking that life-drawing course? What do you think you will accomplish there? How do you feel about drawing live bodies instead of sliced-up dead ones?*

Questioning things went against the grain; reviewing was not a natural act. It was almost as if, after Mama and Papa died, we had decided, without ever saying, that work was our gift: Grandpa his book, the illustrations from me; Piero in medical school; and Prima, with all her degrees and awards, thus far the success of the family. Even Matt absorbed our view: he lived his job.

But the problem was, we were each alone. Loosely gathered. Not one of us had a partner, a lover, someone with whom we shared our life. We were skewed by vocation, top-heavy with work. Our respective lives were more important than our collective life. Time at home was private—to daydream, to stare out windows, to do nothing. It wasn't time anyone could claim.

It wasn't that we didn't love one another, but that our love wasn't shown by domestic acts or by being together. It was shown by leaving each other alone. But was that really love?

Were we still in the swing away from Mama and Papa's

pattern, their calculated and carefully selected life? With them, each round moment was cherished and chosen, made to smell good, taste good, and appear, if at all possible, beautiful. Our parts in their Vuillard interior, their Renoir boating party, their dappled domestic scene, were as silent observers, so as not to interrupt their profound connection, their strange, cadenced dance around the breakfast table, the lunch table, the garden, the tea table—the continuing ritual of their beautiful life.

Would we ever swing back to intense relationships? I didn't know. After Matt, and Toronto, I gave up. Grandpa had always been a mystery, and Prima said she preferred married men. She said they were grateful and undemanding. And Piero, well, he had nurse girlfriends, but he called it mutual need.

None of us gave any sign of being able, or even wanting, to love someone. That was the thing—wanting to. Had we lost the capacity? Quite the reverse. I was beginning to think we'd never had it. That was worse. Something lost could be found again. But something we'd never had? We wouldn't recognize it coming down the road. We'd reject it out of hand, and imagine instead that we were getting a cold. And the worst of it was, when I had my work, I never thought or cared.

Charles waited for me to continue. I couldn't. I didn't know what to say, or how my circumstances were different now, but something had happened. Something about my life had changed. As we walked the brick herringbone sidewalks of Volta Place and the mica-filled sidewalks of Wisconsin Avenue, and then across R Street, past the library, I realized that my work now belonged to someone else's world. I was talking about it and thinking about it and seeing it from the outside, like an observer. It had been taken from me. Bodies were no longer alive. They'd become cadavers. Dead flesh.

Charles could see my gloom growing. I watched him noticing, but didn't care. I was waking from a dream into dull reality; coming from a beautiful, blinding winter snowstorm to indoor shadows. As I watched him climb on the bus, and then watched the bus pull away through a trail of exhaust, I thought about all those years of training, my immunity to the bad parts, the way I could disappear inside my work. I had loved waking up from an afternoon's work to find the day gone, the building shut, the other offices dark and still, and on my table, miraculously—a finished drawing. A gift. It had seemed like magic to me. I had found a way of defeating time. In exchange for my life, I could make bodies immortal.

I walked to the lab. Grandpa's office was empty. In a small adjoining room he kept an old-fashioned dissecting table—a stone slab with carved channels—now stacked with files and journals. Carefully I moved them to the floor. I climbed onto the cool stone slab and lay there, immobile, my eyes closed. I remembered the tombs I'd seen in French cathedrals, with life-sized sculptures of the deceased lying face-up on the lids of their coffins. At the time I had thought it bizarre. It didn't seem so strange to me now.

26 INSIDE

I went swimming every day. I crawled up and down a blue stripe of water until I lost the sensation of moving my body, and only felt a heavy, gentle, dreamlike rocking, as if I were sleeping, or in a trance. I swam until exhaustion peeled over the horizon and then dragged myself home, where the day closed down of its own accord.

I climbed into the attic and found Mama's old terra-cotta pot. I painted the girdle of the female pelvis in gray-white bony paint around its swollen belly. As a small child I had tiptoed into my parents' bedroom and peered into that huge, rosy pot, sniffed the overflowing carnations, and imagined climbing inside and hiding. I had wanted to set up housekeeping inside the smooth, soft shape of the pot, winding my body around the forest of carnation stems. Then, in the night, I could look out from inside the pot to find out what they did in the lace and linen, in the soft layers of cotton and down. What were those sounds, the murmur of voices? And under the floral drift of carnations, what was that salty, musky smell? From the pot I was sure I would understand. All the secrets would be revealed.

The secrets were still here. I could feel them whispering around the house. Every night I dreamed the same dream, again and again.

I am in the house. I hear them coming. I run downstairs to lock the doors, to pull the curtains and turn off the lights. They are crunching over bluestone, up the slate steps, feet by the door. I hear the heavy thud of brass on brass. I wait deep in the shadows. Again the knocking. *I'm asleep, I'm not here. Go away, stay out of my life.* No sound of footsteps retreating on flagstone and gravel. No sound at all. The curtains stir with a warm breeze, with the scent of carnations. Now a woman is standing beside me. Her arms slide around me, I feel her lips on my cheek. A man appears and pulls her away. Damp sounds; shapes and shadows slip through the dark. I close my eyes. I smell blood and carnations. When my eyes open, no one is there. It's almost light. Heavy rain from a summer storm pours in through open windows. The smell of water is everywhere.

What day was it? I didn't know. Not the day of the week or even the date. Did it rain like this every spring—weeks in a row, with no let-up? I'd never noticed before. The city had become a swamp, and my brain a spongelike fungus. When it wasn't raining, the light outside was white and high, with fast-moving clouds. Everything was wet. Roots were swelling. Potholes blossomed. Even the air was rushing here and there like a mad housewife with a broom, whooshing and swatting, stirring eddies of grit and slamming doors. Shutters crashed; drawers hung open. The house felt either too hot or too cold, and full of old smells. Clutter triumphed. Nothing was clean.

I gave up swimming and stayed inside. Lots of days I stayed in bed and didn't come down for dinner. Lilla thought it was too many days. She raised the alarm. When she talked to Grandpa, he called Matt; and before I knew it, they were all trying to fix me.

Matt was in and out of the house almost daily, visiting

Grandpa, helping Clipper. I was used to that. But when it came to me, he used the phone. I knew he was scared. I wasn't allowed to need him. So when he called, I lied. In my strictest voice, I said I was working hard on new drawings; he should leave me alone. He sounded relieved and hung up the phone.

Grandpa thought every problem could be solved with a book. He left Burton's *Anatomy of the Melancholy* open on my desk, with several sections underlined in pencil. I was shocked. He never, ever, marked his books. I copied out the sections he'd marked, and pasted them on the wall above my desk.

Melancholy is . . . the character of mortality. . . . And tis most absurd and ridiculous for any mortal man to look for a perpetual tenor of happiness in his life. Nothing so prosperous and pleasant, but it hath some bitterness in it, some complaining, some grudging; it is all bitter-sweet, a mixed passion, and like a chequer-table, black and white. . . . And he that knows not this . . . is not fit to live in this world . . . there is no way to avoid it, but to arm thyself with patience and magnanimity. . . . For as much as so few can embrace this good counsel, and arm themselves with that patience as they ought to do, it falleth out sometimes that these dispositions become habits, and make a disease. Once grown a habit, it will hardly be removed.

Once grown a habit. He had double-underlined that part. He thought I was indulging myself. Life has lumps and bumps, so what, I should take them, and not get into the habit of moping around. So much for Grandpa's assistance.

After Matt and Grandpa, then came Charles. We hadn't seen each other for weeks. I was sure Grandpa had asked him to come. He appeared one day at the foot of the stairs and shouted my name, again and again, and then announced he was coming upstairs unless I came down. So for the first time in weeks I got dressed and came downstairs.

What did he want?

He wanted me to go downtown. He said I should look at the Chinese art at the Freer. He would be working next door at the Smithsonian Castle, helping to write the catalogue for an exhibit of his father's African gold weights. We could go together. What did I think?

"It's too wet."

"We'll be inside."

"It's too crowded."

He cocked his head to one side. "It's a beautiful building—marble and walnut and empty spaces. It's never crowded."

I was silent.

"I have two months' work. You can come every day. Treat it like a job."

Like a job. I didn't have a job. My job was finished.

"You'll be on your own in the mornings. We'll meet for lunch."

"What about my swimming?"

He paused. "Stop finding problems. Just say yes."

We were standing in the front hall. It was Saturday morning and I hadn't had breakfast, so I invited him into the kitchen for coffee. Lilla was cooking. She pushed us out the back door to cut tarragon for chicken marinade. She didn't want us cluttering her domain. She liked the faint hum of the electric clock on the wall, the refrigerator grunting and wheezing, and the sun slanting through the window. But she didn't like people in her kitchen. It was cool and shadowy, with light like a barn, and lots of open, empty space. The linoleum was speckled green and the counters were a paler green, the old-fashioned color of schoolroom walls. Lilla didn't want a modern kitchen, full of gadgets and brightly lit, with a breakfast nook, or a counter with stools. She liked the brass gooseneck lamp mounted over the sink, and the milk-glass ceiling light, and the small table lamp on the counter.

No one had eaten at the oak worktable in the middle of the room since we were children. On Lilla's day off, we still liked to sit there, drinking coffee and nibbling cake from the Safeway bakery, pretending we were children again, snitching pie dough and drinking milk.

But not today. When we came back with her herbs, we were sent out again with cinnamon toast, slices of melon, and a thermos of coffee—all on a tray.

I didn't realize we could sit in the garden. It was late April.

"Does Matt hibernate in winter, too? I never see him."

"He comes over to visit with Grandpa. They're as thick as thieves." I put the tray between us on the bench.

"Didn't you go away together—travel in Europe? Who told me that?"

I stared across the garden, exhausted by the idea of explaining myself. Clipper saved me. He came into the garden with his hedge shears and a cart. We had finished eating. The coffee was gone. I stood up, and so Charles stood up too.

"See you Monday," he said. "Right here, just after nine." He gestured to the garden bench, and then strode off toward the gate in the brick wall that connected our two gardens. No one had used the gate in years; he struggled with it. Clipper saw him and came over.

Clipper motioned Charles to stand aside. He levered the wrought-iron gate, and as he pried it open, it fell heavily into his arms; the old hinges had rusted through. The two men looked at each other.

Clipper beamed. "High time, Mr. Charles. High time."

27 RENIFLEUR

The first day at the Freer was a shock. I found myself standing in front of a picture of jasmine that looked so familiar I couldn't believe it was in the museum—surely I'd seen it every day. I stood in front of the picture until I remembered, and then felt foolish for ever forgetting.

A museum print of that same jasmine was hanging at home in the upstairs hall, next to a drawing I'd made as a special birthday present for Mama. When I was twelve, I'd drawn one of the jasmine vines that was growing outdoors. I'd showed Papa my drawing. He'd said it was fine, but had insisted I write the botanical name under the picture. He'd said each jasmine had a different smell and a different name. It had to be labeled.

"When I grow up I'll eliminate classification," I'd complained to Grandpa.

"Naming is a form of possession," he said.

"*I* don't care about possession. Naming spoils things."

"Your papa is holding things off with his names. He thinks it keeps the devil away."

I was used to Grandpa's being peculiar, but he rarely insisted I share his views. "Grandpa," I said, "you know there's no devil!"

"*He* thinks there is."

"How do you know?"

"Because he tries so hard to keep him away. If he names everything that comes his way, he'll recognize the devil when he comes along. He even has a name for this garden." Grandpa opened his arms to the yard. "You father calls it a renifleur's garden."

"A renifleur's garden? What's that?" I asked.

Grandpa patted me on the head and looked over my shoulder at the drawing. "Very nice," he said. "But let's not part company with the facts." What had he meant? That he didn't know what a renifleur's garden was? Or that I should label my drawing anyway? Later on, when I heard the expression repeated—renifleur's garden—I assumed, since the garden was Papa's, that it meant a garden with fragrant plants. I assumed the garden was part of his work.

Papa was bossy and Grandpa was odd, but I was used to them both, so I relented and wrote the botanical name, which Clipper supplied from his garden book, along the bottom of the picture. When I gave it to Mama, she hung it upstairs in the hall with the museum print.

When we came back from that first day at the Freer, I ran upstairs to look in the hall, and just as I'd thought, the museum print of Chinese jasmine was hanging beside my long-ago drawing. That it was flattering to hang the two jasmines together had been no consolation. I had wanted mine to go in their bedroom. All I ever saw was rejection.

More and more, I distrusted my memories. They seemed selective—like still shots rather than a continuous reel. Between each image was a blank wall, a missing picture. How much had I forgotten? Or chosen not to remember? What had Papa meant by "a renifleur's garden"? He was calling himself a renifleur. What was the real meaning? I went to the *Webster's Second International* in the downstairs library and turned to *R*. *Renifleur. Renifleur.* There was no listing. Was it a made-up word? Or so old-fashioned it was no longer listed? It was four o'clock. The Georgetown Library was open until six.

It took over an hour to find a citation; I looked in the wrong places. Finally I asked the reference librarian, and she pulled down the unabridged *Random House Dictionary*, turned to *R*, and peered over her half-frame glasses as she read the definition out loud to me: "'Renifleur, noun, psychiatry. One who is sexually aroused or gratified by odors.'" She handed me the dictionary so I could see for myself. "It's from Freud," she said in a cool voice, "but I'm not sure which volume."

Papa was named. He had called himself a *renifleur*. He knew what he was, what he'd done. I remembered Mama's letters, her description of Papa wanting her smell. At the time I'd been more interested in Mama's reaction; that "after he did certain things," she couldn't resist. I didn't think much about Papa's part—about what he had wanted and what that meant about who he was. Papa was right about naming things. What was named became familiar; and what was familiar could never be bad.

Could Grandpa explain this? Would he? When Papa was alive, I always thought the two of them shared some kind of secret. They rarely questioned each other's behavior. Even now, Grandpa never talked about Papa. I could certainly ask, but these days Grandpa was hard to predict. He never said what I wanted to hear, and when he did talk, he made less and less sense—with his Latin quotations and French aphorisms interspersed with archaic medical talk. I would ask Matt. Grandpa had given him Papa's edition of Freud when he started his psychiatry residency. I would walk to his house and look up the reference.

Matt wasn't home, but Marcie said I should look in his study. Freud was always easy to find, a long row of blue-covered volumes. Eventually I found it. What Freud said wasn't so strange—a long quote about the instinctual life of neurotics. Something else was strange. There was a penciled line in the margin alongside the paragraph about the renifleur. Had Matt looked up this citation too? Or was it Papa's mark? I walked home through the damp spring air, more disturbed than I'd felt for a long time.

28 MY CALLING

Every morning, I rode the bus downtown with Charles and then sat in the Freer library reading a book by James Cahill on Chinese painting. At the end of each chapter, I ran up the marble stairs to look at the pictures he'd been describing. Time flew by and I was always surprised to look up and see Charles standing over my table; it was time for lunch. We would whiz across town in a taxi to some restaurant on Seventeeth Street or Pennsylvania Avenue. Lunch downtown was a serious business, which didn't bother Charles in the slightest, but was unnerving for me. The restaurants were filled with K Street lawyers, politicians, and diplomats' wives, all well dressed and looking as if they belonged. My wardrobe didn't apply. I'd never had to dress for my work. After only two days, it was clear I'd have to buy new clothes.

Shopping reminded me of Mama. Twice a year she would take us downtown to Garfinkel's Lilliputian Bazaar. We'd wear white gloves and Mary Janes strapped over white ankle socks. Mama would sail from counter to counter, trailing behind her a dazed, silver-haired saleslady, dressed always in navy blue, her arms piled with underwear, slips, socks, and blouses, always in white cotton; wool jumpers in navy blue or Black Watch plaid; and every year, the same monotonous four pairs of shoes: brown oxfords for school, black patent party shoes with detestable straps, blue Keds (we wanted white), and red leather slippers. There was no variation. The last stop on our annual blitz was the coat department, where Mama would purchase a new Black Watch plaid coat with a velveteen collar, which I would inherit from Prima a few years later.

Mama wouldn't acknowledge synthetics. For us, she only bought cotton and wool. She would lecture us about lisle, pique, lawn, and batiste; weights and weaves, the uses of poplin and gaberdine. Polished cotton was *déclassé*. So were madras and oxford cloth. She said they were common. She deplored nylon and socks with elastic. She would stand by the counter, coiffed and draped in elegant silk, fingering the lace on a silk slip or sighing sadly over a nylon petticoat.

After that first week downtown with Charles, I wandered onto Wisconsin Avenue on Saturday morning, peering into boutique windows, feeling too nervous to go inside. None of the clothes in the windows seemed like anything I could possibly wear. People with uniforms—nurses and mailmen and airline stewardesses—were suddenly enviable. They never had to think or decide. Their anonymous clothes would never stand out or go out of style.

In the end, I did what I'd always done: I asked Lilla. She told me about The Georgetown University Shop, where she used to buy Piero's clothes. She said they had a women's department, and that every year, as she'd walked through, the clothes looked exactly the same. Was that what I wanted? I thought so.

I bought three skirts with shirts to match, a khaki summer suit, a navy blazer, brown stacked heels, and a hemp purse trimmed with the same color leather. No more blue jeans and T-shirts. Everything matched. There was no chance of embarrassing Charles. I looked like everyone else. I didn't admit to myself that I wanted to please him.

It was hard to tell whether he noticed or cared; his manners were that good. He opened doors and walked next to the street and took my arm when we crossed Wisconsin Avenue. He stood up when I arrived or left, helped me with my coat, and offered to carry whatever I was carrying. He made me feel like a special person. He made me feel as if someone cared. But I told myself that his manners were gloss, perhaps even disguise. He was raised to behave that way.

I'd never made conversation before, back and forth, what I thought and felt about random things, but that's what Charles liked. It was hard to do. I kept losing the thread or changing the subject, but never on purpose. It just happened, before I noticed. The problem was, I couldn't listen. And I couldn't find the right words to ask about him.

Charles coped by asking dozens of questions. I thought he was simply being polite. But his questions made me angry. They made me realize that I had no real answers, no understanding, only facts. So I gave him the facts. I would silence his questions by telling too much.

I told him how sad we'd been when he'd left; how we used to imagine his golden box; how it had held our dreams. I told him how Matt and I had gone to the lab; how numb I'd felt about Mama and Papa. I told him everything about Matt: about Venice, about Matt's letter, about how outraged I'd been. I told him how I'd gone to school in Toronto, experimented with men, and then come home to do Grandpa's book. I didn't mention Steve or the drawings I'd made. I was too ashamed. Even so, I felt as if I were handing him an enormous load to carry. I was sure it would drive him away.

"What," he asked, "will you do next? Now that your grandfather's book is finished?" Charles's questions were like depth charges. He didn't mean any harm, it was just his way. He was more curious to know than he was afraid of finding answers. I was the reverse. What seemed an obvious question for him was frightening for me.

He must have known. Of course he knew. Why else would I follow him down to the Freer? I had no work. My sense of vocation had washed away. My "calling," as Julie had termed it, wasn't a calling after all. I felt betrayed by my own behavior. Where was my attachment? I'd been offered jobs at Hopkins and NIH, but wasn't interested. Nothing would be like Grandpa's book. Most medical illustration seemed narrow and overspecialized, reducing the body to electricity and particles. Slides from the molecular microscope were Kandinsky paintings, not Da Vinci silverpoints. Who could care about computer body tomography? CAT scans? Not me. It was nothing to lay my hands on, nothing real, nothing to see with the naked eye. There was no reference that addressed everyone, but only abstraction, man-made images, false impressions, parts without any sense of the whole. There was no context. I wanted my old job back, that was all—that delicious feeling of being involved and taken away. I told Charles I wasn't a scientist. I'd pretended to be one, but really I wasn't.

29 THE EMPTY STUDIO

For the first time in years, I smelled spring. Pollen thickened the air to a yellow haze, and watery light mottled the city with pale fluorescence. I fell in love with the Freer, and with the intricate palette of Chinese painting. Looking all day made me want to work. By the time we got home, I couldn't wait to go up to my room. Charles invited me to swim, but I said no, I would swim later. Old images, from my work in the lab, had been piling up in my mind and transforming themselves. Anatomical forms provided the structure, and with *sumi-e* ink and watercolor washes, I rendered the body as landscape.

Each drawing floated inside a neutral corona of watercolor wash on a vertical rectangle of fine-toothed rag paper: the liver, the cranium, the kidneys, the femur. I transformed what was particular and concrete to something universal and abstract, suspended in Zen space with a Sung palette: charcoal grays, greens so dark they look black, pale peach, flickerings of white, and every possible wash of beige, taupe, almond, and umber. At a distance they were objects; close up they dissolved into colorful, articulate landscapes.

One whole series of teeth—like the rubble of a bombed building.

The vestibule of the vagina—caves by the ocean.

The bony labyrinth of the ear—a curled shell.

Floating finger bones.

The proximal end of the femur—a pale mushroom.

The muscles of the shoulder—dissected and flanged out like exotic sea fans.

The fine tent of the mesentery, ragged and collapsed.

In each picture, organic forms shimmered with the mystery I'd always felt they possessed. What was hidden and allusive had become openly sensuous, and filled with feeling. Very strange.

In the storage rooms of the Freer Library, I looked at scrolls that weren't on display. Each scroll had yards of inscriptions in elaborate calligraphy, as well as a picture. My favorite was called *Dreaming of Immortality in a Thatched Cottage*. It showed a man in a tiny open cottage on a mountainside, sleeping with his head on his hands. As he sleeps, he dreams himself floating above the vast mists and clouds of the mountains: tiny and windswept, sailing over the physical world—transcendent, immortal. The artist who painted that picture identified himself only as "The Empty Studio." When I read his name, I knew someone else had shared my feelings: of things closing down, the road narrowing, the vanishing point becoming clearer and clearer. I was an empty studio too.

30 LAST TO KNOW

"That's it," he said. "The sum of my life." Charles pulled the bell cord. We got off the bus and started walking up Constitution Avenue toward the Natural History Museum. It was our last day downtown together. He wanted to show me the exhibit of gold weights his father had collected while visiting cocoa plantations in Africa.

By his willingness to talk about his life, Charles made me feel there was nothing remarkable about it. On the ride downtown, for the first time, I'd turned the tables: I asked the questions and he answered. He told me he had been married once, when he was nineteen and still at Harvard; he'd had a child who died at three of cystic fibrosis. He and his wife had been too young, unprepared for loss. It destroyed the marriage. His wife became a Wall Street lawyer; he went back to Switzerland and worked for Chocosuisse, where he quickly learned that he didn't want to work full-time in the family business. He came back to Harvard for a doctorate in hydroengineering. He was a free-lance consultant, and worked all over the country. His home base didn't matter. He'd always liked Washington, and when a Chocosuisse office was needed here, he was glad to come and set it up. It was that simple. He had other projects as well: his father's exhibit, and a proposal he'd been asked to submit to the Smithsonian.

These weren't the answers I wanted. Perhaps I was asking the wrong questions. Matters of fact had nothing to do with Charles. Why did that surprise me? Did I understand everyone else in terms of facts? Of course not. I hadn't the faintest notion what made Grandpa tick, or why Matt did what he did, or even who Piero was. Piero the Lucky was what I called him, but I didn't know why. Really, they were a collection of strangers. I took them for granted.

I knew this: Charles didn't spend time running away. While the rest of us were hunting frantically for relief from the round, ordinary relentlessness of every day, Charles took pleasure in daily things. He was nourished by events that no one else noticed—by taking the bus, by the shapes and colors and appearances of things. "Look at the sky," he would say, "how blue it is, against the edge of the Hirshhorn Museum. Feel this marble balustrade, what a lovely curve. And look, that ivy is hanging off the Smithsonian Castle like a lady's dress." On and on. He got high on the world. To him the world was a moving picture show, a source of amazement and pleasure. He made me want to say, *Well, as long as you're looking, what about that woman on the park bench, spanking her baby? What about hunger and murder and cancer and accidents?*

But I knew what he'd say. He'd look at me with his smiling face and talk about art, music, children, poetry. Gardens, families, friendship, fountains. That's the way he was. The glass was half full. He wouldn't let anything spoil his pleasure. He loved life in spite of its slippage.

He made me see myself. For me, the world was something to negotiate around and hold at arm's length. I didn't take pleasure in people and things the way Charles did. It wasn't the facts of his life I wanted; I wanted to know how he'd become who he was, how he seemed to be having such a good time. And I wanted to know what he wanted with me. He was very formal. He touched me only in conventional ways—to hold my arm going across a street, to take a package or help me with my coat. There was never a hint of anything more. Why was he being so nice? The more I told him about myself, the more respectful he became—almost as if he were taking me more seriously than I was taking myself. And he seemed to demand that I take him seriously, too. What did that mean? What did he want? I didn't understand.

Charles took my arm and led me through a crowd of tourists. "It's your turn now," he said. "Tell me more about Toronto."

Toronto. I stared at the cement in front of my feet. It glittered in the spring sunshine. "Okay," I said, "I'll tell you a story." We wove our way through a crowd of teenagers wearing T-shirts saying SPERRYVILLE COMES TO WASHINGTON. Along with spring and the tourists, the sidewalk vendors had arrived in their trucks to sell pennants and ice cream. I stepped up onto the low wall separating the grass from the sidewalk, and as I teetered along, a balancing act, I told him about Steve Gilpin coming into my neuroanatomy lab and leaving a note by my desk. I stopped for a moment and looked across at Charles.

"Formalin destroys the smell receptors. Did you know that?"

Charles shook his head as he opened the heavy door of the museum and ushered me in. He led the way to the restaurant where we could have morning coffee.

I told him how Steve Gilpin had flattered me, made me curious, and then made a speech about my "artistic sensibilities" before showing me the portfolio. I told him how impatient I'd been—to see if the work was better than mine.

Charles interrupted. "It was pornography, wasn't it?"

I looked at him for a long moment and then stared into the distance, remembering that day, and how I had felt. I turned back to him. "How did you know?"

He shrugged. "I just knew."

"I was shocked."

"That bad?"

"No. Not bad at all. In fact, very good. It was the surprise, the shift, the mixing of things: science, sex, death. It was the sudden understanding of what I could do with my skills—if I chose to."

"You were interested," Charles said.

"I was intrigued. I was stimulated. I could feel that too. This is real, I kept telling myself. People are like this. This is the way the world is. I felt stupidly innocent."

Charles's eyebrows went up just slightly. He stirred his coffee.

I told him about Steve, how I'd thought that type of person would come sleazing in with dirty eyes, dribbling spittle, and how surprised I was. I described the apartment, the models, the pictures I'd done.

Charles was silent. He had probably guessed about Steve.

Finally he said, "Were your pictures as good as his prototypes?"

I looked away. After a moment, I turned to face him. "I learned," I said.

He thought I meant I'd learned to draw pornography. It was true, I had. But what I'd really learned, painfully and in great detail, was just how little I knew about love.

"Is this your new project?" Charles asked. "What you're doing in the afternoons that you're so mysterious about? More pornography?"

"No. Just regular pictures. But they're mixed up with all my work. I'm remembering things."

Charles rubbed his face and then pushed back his chair and stood up from the cafeteria table. I gathered my purse.

"It's strange," I said. "As children we never did the conventional things, playing doctor, all that. . . ."

"Speak for yourself," Charles said. "Prima and I had our own anatomy lesson going."

"Really?"

"Sure."

"Why am I always the last to know?"

Charles's voice was light but clear. "That's a very good question."

31 CHOCOLATE

The kitchen was filled with a dark, sweet smell, and for one wild moment I thought Matt was making fudge for our meeting. But as I came in, I saw Piero by the stove, and then Charles appeared at the kitchen door, trailing Prima behind him. I had called a family conference. Prima was in town to give a paper at NIH, Matt had said he'd come, and most important, Grandpa was away for the day at Johns Hopkins in Baltimore.

Charles walked to the stove and peered into four small pots, which Piero was stirring one after another, each with a separate spoon. "You'll be my tasters," Charles said, as he held up a spoon and watched chocolate drip into the pan.

"But I don't like cocoa," said Prima. "It's too sweet."

"All the better," said Charles. "You'll be a good judge." He looked again into the pans and swirled the spoons around in the thick liquid. He had been sent samples of a new cocoa his company was marketing to compete with Hershey and Nestlé. They wanted his opinion. "At least," he smiled, "they *say* they do." He waved a spoon. "I'll go. You want to confer. We can sample it later."

"But I want some *now*," whined Prima.

"You just said you didn't like cocoa," I snapped at her. I looked at Piero. "Who's in charge here, anyway?"

"I'm the oldest." Prima used her professor voice. "Charles may stay if he gives us cocoa."

"Agreed, *chérie.*" Charles bowed, the mock courtier. He returned to the stove and turned the gas back on. I watched his long fingers adjust the blue circles of flame and I wondered, *Why is he calling Prima* chérie? *And where is Matt? He should be here by now.*

As if reading my mind, Prima announced that Matt had called. "He's busy," she said. "One of his people is having a crisis." She sat at the kitchen table, looking pristine and delicate. Technically, of course, I knew what she was: an ectomorph with a small frame. It came down to tiny and bony, a clone of Mama, the same high cheekbones and fine blond hair with wispy curls. She had slim legs, a short trunk, and shoulders that she held slightly forward, as if to be demure about her breasts, which hung like heavy fruit from a delicate tree. But the inner Prima was something else. People who knew her got out of her way. That old cliché of the Sherman tank, crunching over everything in its path. She was as beautiful as a star, and just as remote. No heat. Her eyes glittered but didn't shine.

"We need to talk about Grandpa." I said. "He isn't right. He's becoming peculiar."

"Are you sure?" asked Prima. "Perhaps you've just begun to notice. He's always been odd. He's always talked in riddles and Latin and old-fashioned words—agues and ruptures, all that."

"It's worse," I said.

"Give an example," said Piero.

"I can't, exactly. I mean, it's not one thing, it's . . ." I remembered when I'd asked Grandpa about how Mama and Papa had met. Every girl wants to hear the story of her parents' romance. That I didn't know was typical. Routine facts were taboo in our family. Instead, we knew what we shouldn't have known. When I'd asked Grandpa about Mama and Papa, he had squinted into the sunlight and said, "The child's the father of the man, and all the water's over the dam."

Eventually I'd learned something—but not what I'd asked. Papa had been a resident in surgery at Georgetown Hospital. He hadn't always been a chemist.

"So what happened?" I asked Grandpa. "With them, I mean."

"He met your mother. She was a student."

I sighed. Getting facts was like pulling teeth.

"Your mother was at the Language Institute. Her family was State Department. She'd been living in Paris. Before that in Florence."

"I mean—what happened with Papa and Mama?"

"Well, of course, she was a bit young." He looked away and said, "*Nostalgie de la vierge.*"

"How young?"

He stared at me. "She was sixteen."

"A bit!"

"My dear," he said, "I married your grandmother when she was sixteen, and I assure you, that wasn't *any* too young."

It was the first time I'd heard Grandpa mention his wife. Grandma had always been a mystery. Instead of answering my questions, he ruminated about meeting Grandma—when he was invited to give the commencement address at the Maryland College for Women, in Lutherville, on the Eastern Shore. Grandma was graduating. She had studied vocal music and domestic science. He showed me her yearbook. She was Delta Upsilon, the president of the Thalia Club, and voted Best All-Around Senior. "Ezrina," he said, "the sweetest thing. She smelled powdery."

Powdery. I'd always worn powdery scents; they smelled fresh and clean, like soap and baby nurses. One of the men I knew in Toronto said I even tasted powdery. I still wear that kind of perfume, it comes in a bottle shaped like a crown, and I get it at Peoples drugstore. It's cheap, but I like it. I wonder if Charles likes powdery smells.

Grandma had left Grandpa shortly after Papa was born. I knew that much because Lilla had told me—she'd said something about a gathered breast, whatever that meant, but she clammed up when I wanted details. Grandma couldn't have disappeared. The police would have been called, a report filed, a detective hired. She would have been traced. She must have left with Grandpa's permission. What had happened? I asked Grandpa. He was quiet for a moment and then replied. "It sometimes happens, you know. After childbirth. She wanted her mother. She was melancholy. She wanted to go home." He spoke with no expression. It was a painful subject. So I asked him again about Mama.

"What do you mean, 'not any too young'?"

"A woman needs to be married," he said.

"*I'm* not married."

"An expense of spirit . . ." He pulled out a nail and poked around in the bowl of his pipe. He didn't finish the quotation, but I knew how it ended: "An expense of spirit in a waste of shame." He usually quoted the whole thing—but not about me.

"Your Papa waited until she was eighteen and then they got married. He went into the navy. He wasn't gone long."

"And when he came home, they started a family?"

"Not so fast. When your Papa came back, he didn't want to be a surgeon anymore, he didn't want—"

I interrupted. "Was he in the war?"

"Of course."

"Where?"

"All over, really." He puffed smoke in my direction. "He

was sent to Hiroshima after the bomb. And to Bikini to watch the tests. He was an adviser. He wrote part of that famous report."

"He lost his nerve."

"I never said that."

"You said he quit surgery after the bomb."

"Don't put words in my mouth! I did not say that. I don't pretend to know *why* he changed, or what made him change. I didn't ask, and he never said. Reasons and causes are hard to know, young lady. We can't ask *why* God made a liver or a spleen, we can only describe them and show how they work. That's all we can do. *Il n'y a plus à dire.*" He issued these last comments through a cloud of pipe smoke and then got up from the patio chair and walked inside. End of conversation. Grandpa didn't like to talk about Papa.

"Then what *is* it?" Prima demanded in her most clinical voice.

"His whole self seems off kilter, as if his ballast were gone. He seems to be floating. He's doing odd things and he's talking funny—not the usual medical shorthand, the archaic proverbs, the riddles and rhymes—but all of them, and all at once, garbled together, and out of context, or out of the blue, as if he were speaking a new language or addressing an imaginary audience, or even having a private conversation. Matt used to joke about Grandpa's 'word salad,' but I never noticed until recently how bad it is."

Piero tilted his chair back. "Look," he said, "Grandpa finished his book. And you finished your part of it. You're both in between. It must feel odd to have nothing to do. You're younger, you can cope. But for Grandpa, the book was his life. He has a right to feel at sea. What will he do now? The best part of his professional life is over. And if you must know," Piero continued, "he isn't being any more peculiar than you are."

I glared at him. "Explain that."

"You walk all over Georgetown. You pester Charles at the Smithsonian. You swim. Then you seclude yourself upstairs all afternoon and won't tell anyone what you're working on. Isn't that behavior a little peculiar too?"

"No! Of course not! I'm working."

"Oh!" said Prima. She addressed the group as a whole. "Mona is *working*. Heaven forfend that we should ask on what! Do *not* disturb!"

Piero interrupted. "Don't be nasty, Prima. It's my fault, I changed the subject. We're only here to talk about Grandpa. Mona thinks Grandpa is getting senile. If we must use a word. Prima, what do you think?"

"I think he should go to a doctor. A neurologist could test him—simple as that."

"It's not the truth I'm after. I know what he is, I see him every day. I want some kind of *solution*."

"Solution to what?" asked Piero. "To old age?"

"I mean, the thing is, uh, what will we *do*?"

"Why, nothing, of course." Prima again.

"But he's not himself. He's harder to live with, too. It's not just the way he talks, or that his opinions have become more absolute and fierce. He's almost obscene, in his erudite way. He feels free to discuss medical subjects in any setting: a leg amputation when we're sitting down to a leg of lamb at dinner, with guests, no less; or he reviews his dissection of the vestibule of the vagina and how there was an abscess and what he did about it, on and on. He talks incessantly about military medicine and makes constant references to maiming and dismemberment."

I remembered a recent conversation when Charles had come over to pick me up before we went downtown.

"Well, sir," Grandpa said, addressing Charles. "Did you know that this young lady"—he gestured to me—"came home from Toronto with a specific stomach?"

"No, sir," said Charles, "I didn't know."

"And do you know what a specific stomach is?"

"Grandpa!" I said. He ignored me.

"No, sir," said Charles.

"Hah!" he said, banging his hand flat on the table. "It means she had the Canadian clap." He burst out laughing, and then said: "That's the kind of girl she is. Canadian clap. *Mirabile dictu!* The American kind's not good enough."

For once I was grateful for Charles's manners. He steered the conversation to a discussion of Victorian medical terms, all those words that Grandpa loves: quinsy, dropsy, frights, and fomentations.

When I came home with gonorrhea, Grandpa arranged for my follow-up examination and never said *peep*. But *now* he was talking about it—telling Charles, calling me "a waste of shame." He'd never been judgmental before.

If they could only see. I looked over at Charles and caught his expression before he could change it. He was giving me a pitying look.

"Mona, Grandpa is almost eighty," Piero said.

"And he's not getting younger," Prima chimed in. "This isn't a basketball game where you can call time out." She made the T signal with her hands.

They were talking at me, first one, then the other. I understood their words, but not what they meant. They were driving at something. I stared at Piero. I couldn't believe him. "You don't care, do you? For you it's just, 'Well, Grandpa's getting old, he's getting senile, too bad.'" My voice got higher. "This is *Grandpa*! We're not talking about just any old person. This is, he is—"

"Very important to you," said Prima.

"And not to you?"

"Of course he is. But not in the same way. Don't forget," she said, "I left home. *You* went to the lab, you—"

Piero interrupted. "Mona, the truth is, you're closer to Grandpa. You have a long-standing, everyday sort of relationship. It hurts you to see him getting old, losing his . . ."

"Marbles? Go ahead. Say it."

"You're quite irrational about him," said Prima. "We're all going to get weird and wobbly and lose our teeth and crap in our pants and then, Mona, we are all, every one of us, going to *die*. That's what happens. That's the program. Why can't you accept that and leave him alone."

"It's not the physical part, it's who he is, I . . ."

Piero spread his arms in exasperation and addressed the ceiling. "This whole family handles dead bodies but doesn't accept death. Ever. Extraordinary."

"I can't stand to see it," I said. My voice was small. "I love him." There was a long silence.

Charles got up and started pouring chocolate into cups and passing them around. Suddenly, each of us had four demitasse cups of hot cocoa lined up in front of us on the table. Charles was using Mama's Limoges. He had marked the bottoms of the cups with a grease pencil. Lilla would be furious.

"Very hot," he cautioned.

We sat for perhaps ten minutes, drinking cocoa and feeling rather glum, each of us sipping, and sipping again, and then arranging and rearranging the small porcelain cups in rows in front of us.

"I'm ready," said Prima.

Piero had drunk his, and couldn't remember the last two. "Indistinguishable," he said. "Mediocre."

I sipped mine and looked over at Charles, pain leaking over my face. He looked up from his row of cups. "May I speak?" he asked.

We all nodded and closed our eyes and raised our hands in supplication, as if to say, Sure, why not, anything, change the subject, please, this is terrible.

"Piero, you first, since your cups are empty."

Piero read from the bottoms of his cups: "*C* is first, then *D*. Forget the last two."

"Prima?"

She had memorized hers. But she paused between each letter. "*A. C. D. B.*" She looked over at Piero. "None the same."

I lifted my cups and read out the letters: "*C, C, A, B*. I have two the same?"

Charles grinned at me. He read out his letters. "*C, A, D, B.*"

"Well," said Prima. "I lose."

"Not necessarily," Charles said. "Three of us put *C* first. Prima put it second. Everyone put *B* last."

"May we know the brands?" Piero was licking his spoons.

"Of course." Charles was wearing a jacket. He reached into his inner pocket and extracted a long, buff-colored envelope. He took a knife from the counter and slit the envelope. How like him to use a letter opener. "*A* is Nestlé, *B* is Hershey, *C* is mine, *D* is Droste."

"Droste sounds like a German schoolmaster," said Piero. "Herr Droste, who raps boys' knuckles and takes snuff from a silver box."

"Charles has rigged it so we like his best," said Prima. "What's your chocolate called? Is it that one named after a naked lady?"

"You mean Godiva," said Charles. "No, that's not mine. We're called Chumley."

"Chumley sounds dumpy and English."

"It's meant to. The English love chocolate. It's a big market. But also, Americans are Anglophiles. They like anything that sounds English."

Piero stood up. "Lilla will faint when she sees this mess."

He gestured to the pots and to the drips of chocolate on the table and stove, and to the sixteen tiny cups in four rows on the table.

"I'll clean up," said Charles. "It's my mess."

Prima chimed in. "It was my idea, so I'll help."

I looked from Charles to Prima. She had already tied on a white flouncy apron that made her waist look tiny, and was now standing in front of Charles, holding a chef's apron for him. I watched her tie the strings at his back. Was she moving in for the kill? Prima gave me the creeps. When I looked at Charles, he was staring at me. I excused myself quickly and left the kitchen. I wanted to think about Grandpa. About what I had said. *I love him*, I'd said. I'd said it out loud.

32 UNUSUAL DICTION

Later, up in my room, I decided to call Matt. When push came to shove, he'd know what to do. What did I mean, "when push came to shove?" That was Julie's expression, left over from high school. She'd driven Grandpa wild with her slang. "Your friend has unusual diction," he'd said, stressing the word unusual, in that slightly perplexed tone he adopted when he didn't approve of something. He was sure she'd pollute me. Snob that he was, Grandpa said he could tell by the way she talked that she'd never studied Latin, that she was the type to take Spanish instead. "You know about *that* group," he'd said, raising his eyebrows and sucking his pipe.

But snobbishness wasn't his worst crime. In this case, it was being wrong. Julie was the class scholar. She could sight-read Virgil faster than our Latin teacher, had won the regional Latin prize, and had the highest College Board scores in the whole class. But I never told him. I didn't know what he'd do. I didn't want to watch him back and fill (another one of Julie's expressions). I was also angry. Up to that time, he'd been an unfailing source of truth. I wanted him to know better. And then I felt sorry for him. After all, the way a person spoke used to matter; it was a signpost, like white gloves and those Black Watch coats Mama had bought so religiously every year. None of those old ways of telling about people worked anymore, so I told myself it wasn't his fault. We were all hypocrites anyway. The point was to forgive him for not being perfect.

Was I holding a grudge? Even now, would I not permit him his normal old age? His humanness?

The truth was that while there was no whiff of peculiarity in our exteriors—our family had always appeared clean and clipped and properly dressed—I was beginning to feel that our conventional appearance was a sham, a thin mantle of propriety that, if pierced, would expose something shameful. I felt that our family life had been an elaborate play, and that Grandpa, in his old age, was letting his mask slip. Our real selves were buried under layers of artifice: style, perfume, convention, work. Our real selves were hidden away in our rooms. The rooms contained our secrets.

Grandpa's room, at the back of the house, was filled with old glittery things: a collection of tiny medicine bottles in blue and lavender glass; amber beads; Mexican coins; old-fashioned medical instruments. He had a wooden box full of birds' eggs in their nests, and a skeleton key that opened every door in the house. His room smelled of pipe tobacco and greasy yellow mentholatum liniment, which he smeared on his toes from a brown glass jar; as a child, I had found it both fascinating and repellent. Fundamentally, Grandpa was odd. His best self lived at the lab. When he walked on campus, the cloak of his office fell over his shoulders, and all was well, he knew who he was. But stripped of academic tweeds and distinguished titles, away from his office full of oak files and leather sofas, what was he? More than eccentric. How could I say that? He'd saved me, again and again. He didn't have to be perfect to have my love. I would call Matt. He'd know what to do.

33 BIRTHDAY

Matt was so literal. As far as he was concerned, a party or a present solved almost any problem. "Your grandfather needs a party," he said.

"Nonsense," I said. "There was one for the book, just last fall."

"Not for the book. For *him*," said Matt. "A birthday party, with family and friends. A celebration. He'll love it," he said. "He's going to be eighty."

Eighty. Hard to believe.

Prima came again from St. Louis. Matt came, trailing Marcie and the Bishops, who behaved perfectly—no peeing on the rugs, no scatological whispers about other people's anatomy or what they'd like to do to whom. I invited Charles, and Piero came in spite of being on a surgery rotation, which he was loving, just as I'd predicted. I even wrote to Noel, not with any expectation that she'd come, but with the hope that she'd write or send some small token. And sure enough, the day before the party, a special-delivery letter arrived. Along with congratulations for Grandpa, it brought sad news. Noel was in a sanitarium in Switzerland. She had Parkinson's disease. She hadn't told us before, because she didn't want fussing. I studied the handwriting of the letter. It wasn't hers. She wasn't able to write. I showed the letter to Piero. He hadn't known her, but he was usually kind. It was impossible to imagine Noel incapacitated. She seemed too young.

Lilla asked her sister to come for the day and help with the cooking. Everyone gathered in the drawing room around six. The day before the party, I borrowed Clipper's pruning shears and gathered branches of lilac and plopped them into crocks of hot water in the pantry. By the next morning they were starting to bloom and I filled Mama's blue-and-white Chinese vases with twiggy arrangements and set them on the floor and on the piano and on tables so the whole house smelled leafy, like spring woods.

Grandpa wore his pinstriped suit with his watch chain across his vest and looked slightly diabolical—a wicked, nimble old man who twinkled and stepped lightly and was charming, especially to the ladies. His face was pink and shining, his white hair swept back, and his watery blue eyes darted everywhere, taking it all in. Matt was right. He loved a party.

I had invited people from the university for drinks beforehand, and they came en masse—secretaries, lab assistants, instructors—like a covey of ducks, draped in good clothes and smelling slightly self-conscious, never before having been invited "to the house." They came bearing bottles of wine and small wrapped packages, and I was amused at their mixture of pleasure and trepidation. To them, Grandpa was still perfect. They mistook his old-fashioned language for eloquence, and his eccentricity for style. They were his only remaining uncritical audience, and with good reason. They knew him as someone who had spoken in symposia all over America and Europe, as someone who had been offered a chair at almost every medical school in the country. They felt privileged to know him, and because they had worked with him every day, they were too close to see any changes. Or were they also being polite, like the rest of us?

All evening, Grandpa told stories, the same stories everyone had heard, not once before, but dozens of times. When I'm old, I want someone to tell me straight out, *Mona, you're repeating yourself, I've heard that story six times this month.* So why don't *I* tell him?

Grandpa didn't just tell stories. He larded his remarks with *haec olim meminisse* and off-color jokes and superfluous six-syllable words, garbled together so that it was impossible to know if he was really trying to say something. But everyone humored him, including me. We didn't expect him to make much sense. We acted out of respect and affection, but really, I wanted to say, *Grandpa, pull up your socks. Stop telling the stories about fishing for gar in the Florida Keys and riding freight trains during the Depression; stop saying* mirabile dictu *all the time. Speak English and say what you mean. What* do *you mean?*

We used to have real conversations, mostly about work. He used to confer with Clipper about the garden, and visit with Matt for hours on the weekends. All that had stopped, or at least it was different. The substance of his conversation had disappeared. He never said anything real anymore. What remained was his style—his stories and jokes and funny sayings. Had I missed a clue? Did he want exemption from societal rules? How much exemption? How was I to know?

After the university people left, we had dinner, and then looked at home movies and slides. We'd had lots to drink, or Matt had, anyway. It was easy to tell. He came over and put his arm around me and gave my shoulders a squeeze, and of course there was nothing wrong with that, except what it meant. It meant he still thought about me that way, when he didn't have himself all battened down.

The movies reminded me about Prima and Charles. At fourteen, whatever they'd had going couldn't have been much, but still, there they were, on film, running around the garden and through the lathhouse, into the laundry yard and through the kitchen screen door—slam—out of sight. Into the pantry.

Why did I assume they went into the pantry? Perhaps because it was a cool, dark space full of interesting smells and lovely things. The shelves were lit by jars of paradise jelly and icicle pickles, and by the dull gleam of japanned tins full of crackers and cheese. There were crocks of cornmeal and white flour. Rosemary and thyme hung upside down in bunches to dry. If I'd had kissing in mind, I'd have gone to the pantry, too. But how did I know what they'd had in mind? Or where they'd gone? I just imagined.

I didn't like being reminded of all that, especially now, since Charles had become my friend and Prima was here, wafting around in that way she had. Down at the Freer, I'd seen paintings by Thomas Dewing that reminded me of Prima. Dewing liked painting willowy women—veiled and draped and very romantic. They looked as if they'd been nude in the sunlight and had wrapped themselves quickly in voile or netting or fine thin cotton. There was an unmistakable suggestion of dishabille, a hint of availability. Prima looked the same. Her clothes were like shifts or kimonos, unstructured and easy to unwrap, as if pulling one tie would cause everything to drop at her feet.

The movies continued. There was Prima again, in jerky black and white, the sun splashing white blotches on the film, blotting out faces and background as the camera moved to follow her dashing through the arbor. Then Charles appeared and leered into the camera with an adolescent, clownish look, his dark hair flopping over his high forehead. He was already tall, already handsome in a distinctly European way, and quite sure of himself. He grabbed Prima by the wrist and held up her arm—like the referee in a boxing match. What was the victory? That he had caught her? That she had won? What had she won? I didn't like my curiosity, and liked even less whatever there was to be curious about. Would the movies remind them of unfinished business? Would they decide to finish it?

I was ten when those movies were made—four years younger than Prima. Back then, I'd had no idea what they found so exciting. I'd guessed it was all about kissing and breasts, but I hadn't understood the feelings. I had witnessed the arrival of Prima's breasts the summer before; it had seemed amazing to me at the time, and something I couldn't imagine happening to me. One summer she was flat and solid, the same size from chest to hips, like a telephone pole. The next summer she had a waist and queer little grapefruit breasts, with pink, quarter-sized nipples. Her legs weren't sticks anymore, her thighs and calves had a new shape, and her bottom was high and tight and round like Mama's. I thought she was perfect. I remembered Mama taking her shopping. I wasn't invited. Mama stroked my face and never-minded me with "Your time will come, darling," and promises to bring me something sweet or special from downtown. And she did bring something. She brought me an enormous pink imitation rose, with hundreds of lurid, silky petals. I couldn't imagine a real rose with so many petals. She said it was for dress-up. She also brought chocolates—not from Reeves', down on F Street, where I knew they'd had lunch—but Swiss chocolates in a box with Mont Blanc on the lid. They must have come from Mr. Sylvester. The chocolate connection.

I looked around the room for Charles, to see what he thought of his long-ago image. I saw Prima, sitting behind him, leaning forward over his shoulder, her head so close it was touching his. She was whispering in his ear. He laughed. I could hear her spidery sounds—*psst, psst*—as I got up and moved to the back of the room. The movies ended and Lilla brought out a carousel of slides: pictures of Matt and me in

Italy. There I was, in my miniskirts and sunglasses, lolling over the balustrade of the Borromini Gardens, or dipping my fingers into a tiny village well. The slides of Matt, taken by me, were all out of focus. Back then, I'd never seen him clearly. I left the room and went outside.

34 PRIMA

It was a June evening, still faintly light. Lilla was standing behind the glass patio table, which she had draped in white linen, arranging lovely old Haviland cake plates I hadn't seen in years. Clipper had bottles of champagne in a washtub. From inside I heard laughter and low conversation as the slides changed; outside there was only a slivered moon and the mingled scent of cut grass and brewing coffee. I sat on the bench near the jasmine vine.

Piero came out the French doors and sat down next to me and nudged me with his shoulder.

"Get a load of Prima sinking her fangs into Charles." He waggled his head toward the dining room. "Should be an interesting continuo."

"Shut up."

"Surely you're not jealous? You've kept him at arm's length for the past three months."

I was staring into the shadows. "Envious, perhaps. She's like Mama. Sometimes I wish—"

"You do not. She's as brittle as glass. And about as warm. You think she's disgusting. You don't respect her. If you don't know that about yourself, at least I do." He stared at the French doors. The slide show was breaking up, people were drifting outside. "Poor Charles," he said.

"Charles can take care of himself," I said.

"I'm sure he can—but he's so polite. He puts up with her drama."

"Maybe he doesn't see her that way."

"He's a very sophisticated man, Mona. You know that."

"The nicest men are the first to fall for chiffon and gardenias. Besides, they have a history."

"You *are* jealous." He poked me.

Piero was right. I did like Charles. But I didn't like the way he was making me feel. I gave Piero a look.

His palms went up. "All right, all right." He gestured. "Look."

The candle lanterns on the low retaining walls around the garden beds were mimicked in the upper branches of the dogwood and cherry trees by winking fireflies, the first of the season.

"I have vacation coming," said Piero.

"The beach?"

"Maybe. Charles said I could use his farm. It's in Vermont. Near the Green Mountains. Have you been there?"

"It's a dairy farm. He wants to make fresh chocolates, the way they do in Paris and Belgium. He wants to control his milk source."

"So you *have* been."

"Certainly not. He's told me about it."

"Relax, don't be so prickly." He stubbed out his cigarette. "Coffee smells nice. Can I get you some?"

"Sure."

Lilla was gathering the candles from around the garden to make a circle of light on the patio. The candles in their round jars looked like footlights on a stage, and the rest of the garden—the light night sky and the dark shape of the huge magnolia in the Sylvesters' garden next door—fell away into a backdrop of shadows.

Where was Charles? Where was Prima? I didn't see either of them. Was she reeling him in that fast? I could feel my anger.

Everyone gathered. The sweet scent of blooming magnolia drifted across the patio. I saw Prima in the candlelight. She was holding a huge waxy magnolia blossom in both her hands and breathing in its lemony scent. She dipped her face into the bowl of petals, her mouth slightly open, and held it there. Charles stood behind her. I saw that he was staring at me. Had he seen my look of jealous disgust? I hoped not. I didn't want him to know that I cared. I looked away and allowed myself to be busied with the party. A mound of presents was on the table.

"I'm too old for all this," Grandpa said, gesturing to the presents. "But I suppose that's the point." He bowed to the assembled group. "*Benedictus*, my dear friends. I hope you are sufficiently satisfied with our comestibles, the salubrious weather, the potables, and if you are, there's Madame here to thank." He put his arm around Lilla's shoulders. "And also my progeny, ahh, yes, it was their diabolical plan, they cooked this up. . . ." He went on a bit longer.

Only the regulars were left. Matt had returned, without the Bishops. Charles. Prima. Piero. Some nearby neighbors. Grandpa looked around. He saw he was with family. He waved to the pile of gifts.

"Do I have to open my booty now?"

"Of course not," I said. "Whatever you want."

"I'll open a few."

It didn't matter. Most of the presents were tobacco or bottles of wine, thoughtful gifts that would soon disappear and not require dusting. He picked up a flat rectangular package, and I realized he had chosen my present. There was no card. He would know soon enough.

No one was paying particular attention. Low conversation.

Piero had taken one candle lamp over to the bench and was staring into the night sky. Grandpa began the unwrapping.

"I can tell it's from you." He looked at me. "So wrapped. Hidden."

He opened the paper and lifted the thin tissue paper from the drawing. He stared. He looked over to me.

"Well."

I had given him one of my new pictures. "It's one of a series," I said. "From going to the Freer."

Grandpa looked at the picture for a long moment. I heard him mumble under his breath, "Slay me not by art." More of his Shakespeare. And then, for the first time in weeks, he looked up and met my eyes. "An interesting development," he said. "It has the stamp of excellence."

Charles was looking over Grandpa's shoulder.

"It's not what I usually do," I said, "but it's more than it seems."

"Let me see." Prima drifted into the light. "Humm." She raised her head and met my eyes. "I didn't know you were doing *art*. Matt says you exercise your libido in a swimming pool?" She arched her brows inquiringly and smiled a tight, knowing smile.

I looked up and saw Charles staring at me again.

"Very nice," he said. "Mona's no slouch."

"Oh," said Prima, her voice light, "I never said *that*."

I didn't like Charles coming to my defense. I could take care of myself. My new pictures were very good. That was suddenly clear. They could stand on their own, and so could I. I wanted my pictures admired for the right reasons. Grandpa understood. He knew bodies and he knew art. He was no slouch either.

35 ARTIFACTS

It was past midnight and the party was over. We were sitting around the kitchen table, tired and rumpled. Even Prima had faint shadows under her eyes. With only the gooseneck lamp for light, the room felt like an empty stage, shadowed and cool. Piero had made coffee. Whoever married him would be lucky. He could vacuum and cook and remove spots from carpets and ties. How had he learned? What made him so calm with domestic machines? So serenely in charge in grocery stores? Was it because he'd escaped Papa's rules and opinions? Or was it a matter of being raised by literalists—Lilla in the universe of kitchen sinks and refrigerator deodorizing, and Grandpa in the lab with bodies and bones? For both of them, reality was concrete. As a result, Piero could make decisions about the physical world. He could make coffee or sharpen a lawn mower. He would be a good surgeon. Grandpa called him *Homo practicus*.

While we were sitting, Charles knocked on the kitchen door and marched in without waiting for anyone to get up—we couldn't have done so anyway. He still looked dapper and bright-eyed. He surveyed us.

"A cheerful group." He bent over and pretended to lift my eyelid. "Some of us have overindulged?" I smacked his hand

and Prima rolled her eyes. He put two packages on the table in front of Grandpa. "Your birthday presents."

"I smell a device." Grandpa grinned. "If these are what we talked about yesterday," he said, looking at Charles, "then they're more for the ladies." He pushed the wrapped packages across the table to us. *"Donaria."*

I stared at the tissue paper. "But they're your presents. Do you want us to open them?"

Grandpa grinned again. "Bait the hook well; the fish will bite."

Prima and I exchanged glances. She shrugged. Charles found a cup and Piero poured coffee. Prima undid her package.

"Oh, Lord," she said. "An artifact. Is that right? Am I supposed to recognize this?" She sounded like a child with a chocolate chin who adamantly denies she's been eating cake. "What is it?"

Charles picked up what looked like an elongated shoehorn, only much thinner and made of wood. A bird in the shape of a hook was carved on the end. "This," he said, holding it up, "is a swallow spoon. Also known as a vomiting stick." He handed it to Prima.

She held it gingerly. "Just what every girl needs."

"This one is very old. And valuable."

"And horrible." Prima put it at arm's length on the table.

"Come now," said Charles. "It's a prized object. Rich women collect them. They eat fancy lunches and then—instant diet. It's quite the thing."

"Why did you give it to me?" Prima turned to Grandpa.

"It's a woman's device. I thought you might enjoy it."

"I don't," she said, her voice unpleasant. She glared at him.

I held up the second present. "Dare I? After that?" I motioned to the swallow spoon. Inside the tissue paper was a triangular-shaped bronze object—curved in at its three corners like a sail filled with wind. When I set it on the table, it looked like a miniature alpine tent.

"I give up. Tell."

Prima laughed. "Can't you see?"

"No." I was annoyed. "Just a funny little mound shape."

Prima laughed again. "How perfect. It's a primitive chastity belt."

I looked at Charles. "Is that what it is?"

"It's called a *tanga*," he said. "South American."

"But how was it, I mean—"

"With thongs. See the holes in the corners?"

Prima smiled her vindication. Her swallow spoon looked good next to this. Charles picked it up. "Feel how smooth it is?" He glanced up at me, all the while rubbing his thumb over the bronze curves of the *tanga*. I wanted to hit him.

Piero laughed and said Charles was the best gift-giver.

"There's a reason," said Charles. "Do you want to know?"

Prima gave Charles a warning look. She stood up. "I'm going to bed." She flounced out of the room.

"Okay," I said. "No dramatics. Just tell us."

"My father left them to me in his will—" said Charles.

Grandpa interrupted. "Those objects belonged to *your* father." He pointed to me. "*Veritas, veritas.*"

"To *our* father?" I gestured to Piero and myself.

"*Tuum est. Tuum est.* Over fool's hill. Over it. Yes." He paused. "Your father had a collection of similar, uh, like-minded objects."

"Grandpa! What do you mean, 'like-minded objects'?"

"*Carissima*, what do I mean?" He stroked his chin. "Your father had a collection of devices." He turned to Charles. "Do you think that's an appropriate nomination?"

Charles looked solemn.

"All very valuable, don't you see," he continued, "and interesting anthropologically, but also slightly, yes, can we say, *sic passim*—yes, I think the word applies—perverse."

Charles explained. "My father's will said that Mrs. Emory gave these to him for safekeeping. But since they're museum quality, I think they should be returned." Charles opened his arms. "You see. I was simply returning lost objects."

I looked at Grandpa and Charles. "Not so fast. You're not forgiven," I said. "Either of you."

Grandpa was silent. Charles spoke. "The real question is why your mother gave them away." He gave me a quizzical look.

"I don't want to think about it."

"How strange," said Piero. "You're the one who's always wanting to know the rhyme and reason for things." He tilted back in his chair. "You're the one who's so sure there's a clear answer to things." He thumped his chair down on the floor and buried his face in his coffee cup. In his own way he could be horribly cruel. He didn't seem to have feelings at all. But he was also right. I was backing off.

I held up the swallow spoon. It was quite beautiful. Tapered, and polished with use. I turned to Grandpa. "Where's the rest of Papa's collection?"

"Peccavi, peccavi." he said. *"Raptor, largitor. Argumentum ad hominem, cara puella."*

"Grandpa! Tell me in English."

"A qua bon?" he muttered.

"I need to know."

"A legal request? What is your search, my darling granddaughter?"

"Grandpa! You know I want to find out about Mama and Papa! There's something about them, about our family."

"About every family," said Piero.

"Ours more than most," I said.

"I doubt it."

"Then you don't see. Look at the evidence. Chastity belts and vomiting sticks; Papa sniffing everything and Mama all the time dressed like a Victorian virgin, then every day after lunch, the two of them—"

Piero interrupted. "So what if they liked to screw after lunch? That's not a crime. They took a siesta, it happens all over the world in warm climates. What's wrong with you, anyway?"

"I don't know," I said.

Piero looked at Charles. "She doesn't want to say in front of you. Is this romance?"

Charles turned to Piero. "That's what she's being held back from." He looked directly at me. "Or," he said, "you might call it *love*."

I felt the blood drain from my face. I sat down.

Grandpa stopped stirring his coffee. "Young lady, you're as pale as a pearl." He pushed my head between my legs. As I stared at the speckled pattern of the kitchen linoleum, I remembered the last time I'd felt faint. I was fifteen. I had never dissected or drawn a severed limb before; I was used to drawing internal things, a bone or a sagittal slice of the brain. Grandpa had asked me to draw a hand, and gave me one that was slim and attractive. He wanted drawings of the dorsum, just below the skin, with the fingers flexed in different positions, like those of a piano player, to show different extensions of ligaments and tendons. While I was drawing, I imagined the hand playing Bach inventions, and then felt my face go hot and clammy. Grandpa happened to be in the lab. When he saw my face, he pulled smelling salts from his vest pocket.

"I've been carrying these for years," he said. He peered at the label after recapping the bottle. "Not," he said blandly, "that people haven't fainted before." He patted my back. "Are you pregnant?" he asked.

"Grandpa!"

"Don't be offended. Every medical student who's ever fainted in the lab was in her first trimester. It's a labile time."

So here we were: Grandpa to the rescue again. He stood up and went to the pantry. "Let's have some brandy," he said. He came out with a green frosted bottle. He unstoppered the cork and sniffed. Piero found clean glasses on the drainboard and Grandpa poured.

36 POSTMORTEM

Grandpa finished his brandy and excused himself. Piero stood up with his glass. "Let's toast to Charles. The post-Freudian hero!" He pulled Charles to his feet.

"You're joking!" I said. "What does that mean?"

"A post-Freudian hero is in charge of his conflicts. He knows his soft spots. Everything is conscious. There's no tragic flaw. The tragedy is life itself—its situations, its dilemmas, all that. . . ." Piero waved his hand. "It's no longer a matter of carrying the seeds of one's destruction in one's personality, like a time bomb. There's only choice and will."

"Sounds scary," I said.

"Perhaps," said Charles.

"But not to you?"

"I never claimed the part. In fact, I'm not sure it exists."

It was late. I was angry at Charles. I started to talk about him as if he weren't there, and he, in turn, stared out the window into the black night, his legs crossed elegantly.

"Charles has no conflicts because he flits around, a little of this and a little of that."

"Oh, deliver me," said Piero. "More of the family ethic. Work and pain, hand in hand."

Charles turned around and looked at me. "So. You think I don't do anything."

"You do too many things. You're all over the map. Exhibits, chocolate, dairy farming, swimming pools. Remember your Kierkegaard: 'Purity of heart is to will one thing.'"

Charles uncrossed and recrossed his legs. "On the grounds of having too many interests, I'm weighed and found wanting?"

"I didn't say that."

"You just did." He turned to Piero. "Didn't she say that?"

Piero shrugged. He knew better than to get caught in the crossfire. "I'm leaving," he said. "All of a sudden this got too serious."

Charles stood and shook hands with Piero, and then sat back down.

"You could leave too," I said.

"No," he said. "We need to fight."

"This isn't a fight."

"I see."

"You do *not* see!" I tried to make my voice sound more reasonable. "Listen. I don't like you being so moderate and so interesting at the same time. It offends my view of how things are. You're supposed to be spoiled and impossible." I stood up and walked around the kitchen, touching things here and there. "I don't like you knowing all the time what you want to do and to what degree. Today a little chocolate, the jet-set executive tomorrow, and the day after you're dairy farming, talking milk yields and fat content; it's all too much."

"Could you be jealous?"

"Jealous of what? Your dilettantism? Your lack of focus and direction? Of that?" I said, shaking my head.

"No." He paused. "That I'm enjoying myself."

"Don't be ridiculous. Listen," I said, trying to hold a reasonable tone. "Real pleasure, for me, comes with doing one thing and doing it well. That's all I know."

Charles sighed. "We have one life. Then nothing. Our picture might be in an album somewhere, but in a hundred years no one will remember who we were or what we did. No one will care. Life should be enjoyed. Not rushed through. I can't worry that much about achievement."

How strange this was. I looked over at Charles, at the person he had become, whoever that was. He smiled at me—a rangy, dark, handsome smile, his face slightly irregular, unlike the symmetrical features I associated with American steak-and-potatoes healthiness. Just at that moment, I wanted to load him with the conventional baggage Americans associate with Europeans: tradition, class consciousness, mystery, irony. I wanted him languid, seductive, unimpressable, and consummately wicked. I wanted him to have no values to speak of, and no beliefs except in the completeness of his sophistication. And I wanted to take him on—no strings attached, the way I'd taken on men in Toronto—just for fun. It was my old way of coping with men. And it wouldn't do now. I liked him too much.

"You're too American," I said. "Bright-eyed and bushy-tailed. Full of plans and values."

"What's wrong with that? I came with things to do: the chocolate office, the exhibit catalogue, the pond project."

"The pond project! Sounds like a thriller. No. Let me guess. You're going to count all the ponds in New England?"

"That's a good idea. I wouldn't mind."

"You're going to *build* a pond—from scratch?"

He gestured thumbs-up.

"For the Smithsonian? Right? You see—I'm beginning to know you!"

He smiled. "I didn't know you were trying."

I got up to take my glass to the sink. "It will take forever."

"It's supposed to."

"I meant the pond."

"Oh," he said lightly, "is that what you meant?"

There was a long silence.

It was past two. Outside, the sky was thick and gray. Charles uncrossed his legs in that way he had.

"May I call you by your real name?"

I shrugged.

"But does it apply? Pomona of the myth, wooed by all, but always resisting?"

"Have you been talking to Matt?"

"I asked him if he had a claim."

"What did he say?"

"He said you're a true Pomona. Arm's length. Was he telling me you're involved with him?"

"He's unfinished business. He bothers me."

Charles got up from his chair and circled the room. He put his glass in the sink. "May I see the rest of your new drawings?" He took my arm and we walked to the hall and up the stairs.

In my studio, he went to the window and looked across to his house, and then down to the dark garden. The sky was a lighter gray. I went to my files and opened a drawer. He came over and stood beside me, so close I could feel the warmth of his body. He smelled of pine. We went through my pictures.

"These make me feel better. More free," I said.

"I didn't know you were interested in freedom."

"I'm content."

"No one is perfectly content."

"That's untrue."

"You're afraid."

I turned to him. "I want to draw these pictures"—I gestured to the open file drawers—"and to start my regular work again. I want to work and be left alone. That's all."

"Pomona?"

I said nothing.

Finally he said, "Are you very sure that's all you want?"

I sat down. I didn't speak. I didn't know why I felt so angry. I thought about Grandpa, about how it felt to feel connected. I thought about Matt. I looked at Charles. He knew too much about me. He was pushing too hard—with his peculiar gifts and his persistent questions. And yet, for weeks we had been arranging our lives around one another, without saying anything about it. We rode buses, took walks, went swimming, ate lunch. I was always wanting to be near him. Each morning I felt pulled into the garden, no matter how hot it was, because I knew Charles would come out too, and we'd sit together, synchronizing the day to include one another. I closed my eyes. When I thought about Charles my chest got tight.

I stood up. "Look at me. I'm twenty-eight years old and living at home. I'm not like you. I'm very different." I moved across the room. "I'm angry all the time and I don't know why." I touched the frame of the window. "You can't push me. It won't help."

Silence. The sound of birds outside the window. Charles walked to the door. He turned around and started to speak and then stopped. I heard him going down the stairs and out the front door.

I sat on my drafting chair and was suddenly tired. I didn't trust myself to feel. I wanted to care about Charles in a clean way, in the honest way I loved Grandpa and loved my work. I wanted to be fresh with him, like a new piece of paper, blank and full of possibility. It didn't seem possible.

37 THE BEACH

Each summer, Matt moved his household to Rehoboth Beach to stay in the same old porched house we'd visited as children. Grandpa and Piero went too; it was a regular thing they'd been doing together, ever since Matt started his house. When Matt first took his people to the beach, I was appalled. Wasn't he asking for trouble? I asked. Didn't he do enough already? To which Matt replied, "Perhaps if they'd had vacations before, they wouldn't have so many problems now." He talked about the restorative properties of sea water, about exercise as a remedial agent. He'd adopted Grandpa's Victorian views.

"Did you know," he said, ignoring my doubts, "that Marcie had never seen the ocean? That Hiram doesn't know how to swim? He doesn't even know the world is round. This is an adventure for them." His eyes widened.

"They're children," I said. "And you're being the Good Mother. They'll love you for it."

He wouldn't react. He knew I was jealous. When I grouched to Grandpa about Matt and his people, Grandpa said that if I didn't see, he couldn't explain—on and on about received knowledge.

They left in time for the Fourth. I watched the car pull away from the curb and then slammed outside to water the garden. Clipper and Lilla were on vacation and I was in charge. It all seemed an enormous nuisance. I sat down on the garden bench.

Charles understood that the garden was our meeting place. Going outside to turn on the sprinklers was my way of saying I wanted to see him. But I hadn't seen him since Grandpa's party. Was he leaving me alone on purpose? Had I scared him away? He had called to say he had work in New York. I was welcome to use his pool.

It was horribly hot. I kept seeing myself at the beach, being pushed around by thick dark waves and scoured by sand. I wanted that constant offshore breeze to empty my mind of feelings and wishes. I should've gone with Grandpa and Matt. Why hadn't I gone?

I knew why. With Grandpa's book to finish, I'd had an excuse, but now I had to admit the truth: going to the beach with Grandpa made me uncomfortable. He revealed an aspect of himself that frightened me. Stripped of his tweeds and pipe-smoking silences, he became unnervingly corporeal. Every day he wore baggy beige swimming trunks and an unbuttoned white cotton shirt, both of which exposed more of his flesh than I wanted to see: a bloated white belly, like a huge dead fish; thin white legs; and, when he sat down, globular blue-veined testicles oozing out from inside his shorts. He wore a misshapen straw hat, fringed at the edges and stuck full of feathers he found on the beach—those feathers Mama would never let us collect. She was sure they had lice.

Every beach community had someone like Grandpa, stalking along in a weird hat, leering at pretty girls and frightening toddlers, making teenagers laugh and point, and mamas shift their eyes in disapproval. Grandpa became that person when he went to Rehoboth. He took his hat and his uncovered body everywhere, and as far as I was concerned, he was no longer Grandpa. He became someone I didn't want to know.

By staying home, I didn't have to acknowledge Grandpa's unbound self, the Grandpa who ate lime sherbet cones for breakfast and hung around Dolly's to watch pretty college girls making taffy. I preferred his laboratory persona: constrained, scientific, scholarly, almost unintelligible in a way, but very secure, very dependable. Someone I could count on.

Charles must have been standing there for several minutes before I noticed him. He was back from New York.

I stood up. I looked at the planes of his cheek and jaw, his dark hair. How strange to have known him as a child, to see the changes.

"I've been abandoned," I said. "Everyone has gone to the beach."

"You weren't invited?"

"It's always been something of a men's club. Usually I don't mind, but this year feels different."

"I'm leaving too."

I couldn't blame him. We were in the middle of a heat wave. Each day was a blast furnace. The sky was white, the garden glittered like a green oven, and the humidity was suffocating.

"I'm going to Vermont to check on the farm. And to see some ponds."

I looked at him accusingly. Defector.

"You know you're invited."

"They've left me in charge."

Charles stared at me with a pained expression.

"It's not just the garden," I said. "It's everything." I waved my hands at my surroundings. "It bothers me how little I understand about the people I grew up with. Grandpa and Matt know things I want to know, yet they refuse to tell. It's their way of keeping me home. The implication is that on some future conditional day, if I become the right sort of person or develop the right sort of attitudes, then and only then will they tell the secrets they know."

"I was there," said Charles. "I knew your parents."

"I don't want opinions. I don't want stories. I want facts. Primary sources."

"Like your father's collection?"

"I suppose. And all that stuff in the attic."

Charles gave me an assessing look. "Do you really think it's a matter of facts?"

I shrugged. It was clear that he didn't think so.

"Mona," he said, "do you remember my golden box? The one I never opened?"

I nodded.

"That box was empty. There was nothing inside; it was simply an old chocolate box."

Right then I knew he was like the rest. He knew more than he was saying. But about what? If understanding was not a matter of facts, what was it? Was he saying my parents were like the box, entrancing and glossy on the surface, but inside, nothing—a mystery that could never be known?

I could find out for myself. I didn't need to be taught and told. No one had taught me to draw. I'd taught myself. But that was different—I *wanted* to draw. Did I *want* to know? Silence. Yes. Finally, I wanted to know.

38 CLUES

I was alone. The house was shut up like a tomb against the heat, but even so, my room was unbearable. Washington itself felt oppressive, not just with the stifling heat, but as a place to be, a place to live and conduct my life. For the first time I wanted a place of my own. My rooms upstairs were not enough. My only refuge was the lab, a room adjoining Grandpa's office. I was not detached. Every place I had was adjunct. I felt harnessed to these men, to this old house, to the garden, the neighborhood, the lab, the swimming pool. I felt squeezed into my parents' life. It was claustrophobic and suffocating, like the heat wave that hung over the city.

I listened to the fans swishing and whispering around the shadowy house and I imagined someone, some family member, whispering secrets.

Every day I searched for clues. Even with the attic fan going, I could hardly breathe on the third floor. It was the usual jumble: trunks, boxes of old tax returns, tennis rackets, the requisite dress form—was it Grandma's? Or was it Mama's? Was that her shape?

I pulled the dress form out from under the eaves—a tiny-waisted, deep-chested, hourglass figure. It must have been Mama's. I opened a trunk. It was filled with clothes, neatly folded: gloves, scarves, purses, shoes. Even now they smelled of Mama. A faint drift of floral perfume. It was the accessories trunk. I opened another. From under layers of tissue and heavy brown dry-cleaner paper, I extracted a fine white cotton shirtwaist with a full pleated skirt. I pulled it over the dress form, tugging here and there to get it in place. I buttoned the front. It needed a hat. I grabbed a hockey stick, pushed it into the neck hole, and balanced a brimmed felt hat on top. It didn't match. Too wintry. I burrowed in the trunk. Yes. A straw hat. With a ragged white ribbon and a shallow brim, turned up in the back. I moved back for a better view and bumped my head on the rafters.

"Mama?" I said. "Is this who you were? Remember me? Remember Mona?" Silence. The faint breath of the fan brushed at her skirt. "Mama," I said, "were you ever alive? What did you feel?"

Through the dust and the gloom and the thick, dirty heat, I heard a faintly ringing bell, a sound with no context, like the first disorienting noise of a morning alarm clock. It was the telephone downstairs, ringing and ringing, waking me from my dream. I thumped down the attic stairs into the cooler shadows of the house. I was sweating and my hands were covered with black dust.

It was Matt. I was surprised. I was the one who usually called.

"There's a drought," I said. "I have to water every day." I looked at the dirt on my hands and rubbed them together, holding the phone against my ear with my shoulder.

"Have you decided yet about a job?"

"I'm leaning toward NIH."

"That's good. Are you swimming?"

"Why so uncle-ish? I cadge invitations to swimming pools. We've been to the Harrisons' twice."

"We?"

"I invited Charles."

There was a pause. His voice changed. "Everyone here is

fine. Hiram's mad for the water. Marcie was terrified at first. Wouldn't go to the beach. I'd forgotten how noisy it was. The sound frightened her."

"But don't they love it?"

"Absolutely. Tildy's eczema is gone. We're brown and healthy. Of course, Marcie is ga-ga about the men. I found her under the boardwalk last week with three guys. I came back with a policeman—they should know better, it's obvious she's not normal."

"All your babies," I said. There was another pause. I waited.

"Mona," he said, "we're coming home early. August tenth."

"But why? It's so hot. What's the matter?"

"I have to work on my paper for the APA meeting in September."

I remembered Grandpa. "Is something wrong? Is Grandpa all right?"

Matt laughed. It was good to hear. "He's fine. His usual self. I just wanted to let you know. We'll be back on the tenth."

"You'll boil," I said. It was mid-July. "I've been wanting to leave, myself. Charles invited me to Vermont." I shifted the phone to my other ear. I didn't say that Charles had already left.

"When?"

"When what?"

"When would you go?"

I rubbed my hands together again, and tiny balls of black dirt fell to the floor. "Oh, I probably won't. I have to take care of the goddamned garden."

I didn't usually swear. Matt registered his disapproval with silence. Fuck you, I thought. Mind your own business.

I thumped downstairs to turn on the sprinklers. The outdoor thermometer on the patio said ninety-six degrees.

39 THE GARDEN

Each day I ransacked the attic. But the things I unearthed were commonplace. Noel's books, torn and tattered, were, on rereading, embarrassingly dated; Mama's box with the bas-relief lid, tarnished black, was much smaller than I remembered and only silverplate after all. Her beautiful things had disappeared. I never found Papa's collection. No single object would bear the weight of my expectations.

Evidence, artifacts—what did they mean? What could really be known about families? Was Papa a lecherous boor, ravishing Mama every afternoon against her will? Or was Mama a professional victim, holding it up to him day after day: *You never really touch me, you can't make me feel.* Did she enrage him this way? Or was she the legitimate prisoner of a wicked, two-faced man? The gentleman and the pervert. Or perhaps it was something else. Perhaps they were really in love.

Who was I to talk about meaning, as if facts could clear up my clouded view? But what was the clear view? That Papa collected odd anthropological artifacts? That he made Mama use them? And during those long spring and summer afternoons when Mama and Mr. Sylvester would say *Now run along, dears, while we talk about books,* and we ran along, just as they asked, who knew what was really happening upstairs in that beautifully paneled, book-lined study on those long leather sofas? Did they spend the afternoon in the books, as they said? Or in other pursuits? What was real? I had never wanted to know. Not really.

After each morning of unsatisfactory rummaging, I tried to work. It was humid as well as hot, and when I swept my hands over my work to brush away bits of erasure, my lines smeared, my paper stuck to the board, everything was limp, blurred, and unclear. Each day, after several attempts, I balled up my papers and stomped downstairs.

It was Saturday afternoon. Outside, on the sidewalk, Georgetown was empty. Congress had adjourned, the university summer session had ended, and those who hadn't left for the summer had at least decamped for the weekend. I walked around, looking at houses with signs out front saying ROOMS FOR RENT. It was a buyers' market. The Georgetown students wouldn't be back until fall.

Walking down Wisconsin Avenue, I passed through drifts of city smells: rotting gutter wash from the back doors of restaurants, hot macadam, diesel oil. Each sensation overflowed with memories of my parents. They had been the arbiters of my existence. They had owned the roses, the dapples on the sidewalk, the scent of melons and strawberries, the joy of clean cotton, cool showers, sleep, dreaming. Every sight and smell was loaded with reference. There was meaning in the mown grass and the glittering heat. It was a child's view, an old view that would have to yield. I had to reclaim these things for myself. To live in the present.

Back home, I dragged myself into the garden to turn on the sprinklers. I looked at the flowers with loathing. The draping wisteria and clambering roses smelled cloyingly quaint, a parody of a cottage garden. No, the garden was more than parody. The garden embodied my parents. The garden was fraud. It was as forced as funeral flowers, with that too-sweet, almost rotten smell, a floral convention used as disguise—a complete sham. And yet I was still here, sitting exactly where I'd sat years ago as a child with my artist's book of blank paper and my tin box of watercolors. I'd sat miserably on the garden bench and looked up at my parents' window. I saw the silk curtains blowing in the summer sunlight and averted my eyes. I didn't want to know. But now I did. The scent of jasmine crept into my mind and reminded me of something I could only imagine—not these horrible flowers, so feathery and intricate, with their scent the strongest thing about them—something else.

Walking around front to the portico, I had to give myself instructions—take this step, take the next—as if my body were separate from me, an awkward, stumbling, drunken thing. I went in to bed and lay on top of my sheets, stiff and seething. I wanted to yank Mama from her grave, wherever it was, and yell: *You were a fraud, Mama. But if you were a fraud, so am I. What's wrong with me, Mama? I feel dead, like you.*

I don't remember getting out of bed. It must have been just before sunrise. I don't remember going to the shed for the sharp-beaked, long-handled pruners, but I do remember with absolute clarity the pleasure of the first cut, a crisp slice, clean and taut, and then the crashing sound of the wisteria vine, pulling the arbor down as it fell.

I moved around the garden with deliberate, almost mechanical concentration. I ripped the jasmine vines off the trellis, smashed their pots, scattered the dirt. The lilacs took longer, hundreds of stems, some thick, some thin, all leaf and twig, requiring endless snipping until my arms ached. As I sliced and sawed at the flowering crab, huge branches fell at my feet until only a naked tree trunk remained. I went for the ax and chopped steadily until there was only a hacked stump surrounded by heaps of leafy branches. I popped the small azaleas out of the ground and threw them in a heap; the larger bushes I upturned with a garden fork, slicing at the root balls with the sharp edge of a shovel. In the perennial border, I yanked out day lilies, chopped at soft mounds of artemisia, pulled up rosebushes, trampled over peonies, dianthus, campanula, hacked up clods of earth with a hoe, exposing hidden colonies of bulbs in the process.

The whole time, as I forked up bulbs and unearthed mounds of asters, I raged at Mama and Papa. I would never know who they were. It wasn't possible. But one thing was sure: they weren't who they had pretended to be. They never had been. That was the truth about Mama and Papa. I hadn't wanted to see it.

I was wearing shorts, sneakers, and a T-shirt—none of which I remembered putting on. By eight in the morning, when I finally stopped, my arms and legs were scratched and bloody, my face smeared with dirt and sweat. I leaned on the hoe and looked around. I had leveled the garden. It was such a relief.

40 DESIGNED TO BE WATCHED

It took a week to finish the job. I worked each morning for two or three hours, and again after dinner. I told myself it went so fast because Clipper kept the tools sharp, or perhaps because I had been conscientious about watering. I had expected resistance. I wanted to wrestle with roots and vines, and was prepared to dig and chop for the rest of the summer. But to my great surprise, the garden was shallow-rooted, soft-leaved with scent and display. There was nothing substantial holding it there.

On my last day, as I was tying up branches, Charles appeared by the wrought-iron gate, surveying silently all I had done.

"I'm grateful," he said.

I didn't understand.

He gestured to his magnolia, its huge branches spreading over the wall and into our garden.

"What did you find?" he said.

"Nothing," I said. He had been right all along. What I'd discovered was not a matter of facts.

Charles came over and took the garden twine from my hand. "Do you remember," he said, "how your mother and my father used to talk for hours with books spread out over the rugs, how we played in the garden while they had tea?" He sat on the garden bench, amid the wreckage I had created. "Don't you remember how it suddenly stopped?" Charles looked across to the patio. "How we moved away?"

"And Prima was sent away."

"What do you mean, 'sent away'?"

"That's how I've always thought of it. She went to boarding school. I always felt she'd been dismissed. I was afraid it would happen to me. I didn't want to be sent away."

Charles shook his head, as if talking to himself. "I was forbidden to use the upstairs sitting room. And I was banned from your house. Your father didn't want me playing with Prima."

"I never knew that."

"The gate was locked. Don't you remember?"

I got up to spray my hands with the hose, and then rubbed my wet hands on my face. Our two houses had always been connected—first by the wall, which was jointly owned and maintained, and then by the gate, which opened in both directions. For years the gate had been locked, but since Charles had come home, it was kept open.

Charles stood up. "Come with me." He pulled me off the bench and walked me through the iron gate, past the magnolia, and along the brick path to the front of his house. We went through one set of doors, then another, and up the carpeted stairs. He said nothing. The house was unchanged. I used to take these steps three at a time, and slide down the banister when no one was looking. I was often asked to go to the kitchen for more hot water for the teapot, or sometimes I carried a tray with slices of lemon cake and tiny iced petits fours.

On the upstairs landing we turned and walked through heavy double doors and into the wood-paneled parlor. This was the room where we'd had our teas—the room from which Charles had been banned. He had brought the same old furniture out of storage: Oriental rugs, leather sofas and chairs, and inlaid tables with elaborately turned legs. Two large windows came down to the floor and opened onto small wrought-iron balconies that looked across and down into our respective gardens. The windows were draped with velvet in long green folds.

"I don't remember the drapes."

"They weren't there. My father had them put up. I had new ones made when I moved back." He walked to the window and pulled the drapes aside. I stood beside him. There was a view of the remains of the garden and, above that, the entire side wall of our house.

"Look," said Charles.

"What do you mean?"

"Look at your house."

I looked. I saw the two second-story windows that faced the garden. It was my room. My parents' room. And today, just as before, the windows were open, and I could imagine the white curtains blowing, just as they had twenty years before, in the spring breezes.

"They could be seen," he said.

"You mean—after lunch?"

"Yes. Then."

I looked at him and then out the windows. I ran my hands along the velvet drapes. "Did you see?" I asked.

"Once. With Prima."

I stared out at the nonexistent white curtains blowing, and finally turned to Charles.

"My father had these drapes put up, but still, we could sometimes hear." He paused. He turned and met my eyes. "Mona. It was designed to be watched." Charles went to the door. "I'll get us something to drink." He disappeared.

I stood up. "It doesn't matter," I said. "I should leave." I sat down again. It shouldn't matter. It didn't matter. I waved my hands in the air. I needed something real.

41 BOILING BONES

Six blocks away, on Q Street, on the second floor of a small frame house, I found three white, empty rooms. They smelled of roach spray and fresh paint, but there were seven windows, all facing north. It was a beginning.

Charles helped me move. The shock was how little I owned: my drafting table, lamp, and chair; a few cardboard boxes of books and equipment; file drawers and a suitcase of clothes. That was all. The previous tenant sold me his doormat and air conditioner.

As I carried my things up the stairs, I remembered how often I'd complained to Julie about my parents' house—how old-fashioned it was, full of heavy, dark Victorian furniture, faded rugs, Chinese lamps with fringed shades. Back then, it had seemed that everyone's house was furnished in Danish Modern, with shag rugs and shiny, bullet-shaped lamps. Julie's mother had a glass teapot, and cantilevered chairs of woven leather. Back then, I'd decided my house would be sleek and polished, furnished with metal, glass, and plastic. Instead of wrought iron and teak in the garden, I would have director's chairs. Instead of Mama's painted Hungarian china, I would buy plastic insulated cups and turquoise aluminum glasses. I would replace Lilla's homemade molasses cookies with white sugar candy from the drugstore. I'd wanted trash. It had seemed more real.

But now, in my new apartment, I felt an acute desire to recreate the atmosphere I was leaving: the overstuffed chairs, the golden, almost Venetian light that suffused the parlor, the soft colors of the faded Bokhara rugs. I told myself it was simply a matter of familiarity. Of a known place. That I was frightened of change.

Summer dragged on. Piero came home from vacation and went back to his grind. When I explained as much as I could—about the wrecked garden and about my move—he pulled on his bottom lip and said, "You were always the one to carry our grief."

Weeds grew up in the garden. Beer cans that passersby threw over the wall went uncollected. Clipper and Lilla came back from North Carolina, and without a word, Clipper called a trash company to haul away the stacks of bundled branches and rented a small tractor to pull the stumps. Otherwise, he left it alone. A yard of weeds.

In my new apartment, I slept badly and woke each morning drenched in a cold sweat. All my life had been reaction. Reaction to the white silk curtains, to my parents, to the bodies in the lab, to Matt, to Venice, to my own body—to this, that, the next thing. Even destroying the garden was reaction. It was, after all, an innocent thing. But to me, the garden embodied my parents. Their invented life. The life I had helped to invent.

I started looking for a gallery for my Freer drawings, and took a part-time job illustrating surgical techniques for detached retinas. Since my life seemed such a shifting morass, I wanted something familiar as ballast.

A lab had always been a place where mysteries were revealed, where what was unknown could be discovered.

That had changed. A specimen was no longer a secret; it

was a section of tissue, fixed in time. Objects that had been intricate puzzles stayed irritatingly literal, almost mundane.

What was that quotation from Tyson that Grandpa had used in the front of his book? *I have made it my business more to find out the truth, than to enlarge the mythology.*

I misunderstood Tyson, and why Grandpa admired him so much. Edward Tyson had wanted to find out what *could be known*. He hadn't studied anatomy as a substitute for discovering something else.

What was I doing at that lab with Grandpa? Taking my parents apart? Trying, like the greedy, curious farmer who killed the goose to get the golden eggs inside, to see how the loving business really worked? In a way.

I learned technique, I had the talent and the discipline, but in the long run it wasn't sufficient. The lab was a place of facts. I couldn't dissect my imagination.

In the medical school there was a place where they boiled bones and prepared skeletons. I'd found it one day by accident when I was sixteen. I smelled a dry chemical odor and wondered, *What's going on here?* I saw a huge kettle, the kind used in institutional kitchens, and lifted the lid. Inside was a grayish soup of bones, small ones, from hands and feet, rolling around, chattering in the pot. There were one, two, several pots, on separate burners. I circled the room, lifting lids, peering into uncanny cauldrons: skulls with lower jaws detached, swirling around; patellas, ankle bones, the twenty-six bones of the hand.

I remembered something Grandpa had said. Boiling human bones had been forbidden—when was it? In the Renaissance? In Bologna? The church placed a ban on boiling bones. They wanted the whole body buried. I would do the same.

42 ABEYANCE

Grandpa didn't say anything about my moving out, but when I came over for dinner his first week home from the beach, we walked through the waist-high weeds in the garden and he said to me gravely, "You must live within your harvest."

Was he talking about me? Himself? Both of us?

I hadn't known he cared about the garden. I hadn't considered Grandpa at all. Some kind of amends had to be made.

Every afternoon I went to the Library of Landscape Design at Dumbarton Oaks, where, in a quiet, high-ceilinged room, with books piled on a long oak table, I looked at pictures of gardens.

Like nature, I would plant in the fall: Russian olive, cypress, and pyramidal yew. Laurel and box. Ivy, pachysandra, and spiky tufts of lily turf would replace the grass. It would smell clean and resinous. I ordered pear, fig, and quince, to espalier along the brick walls; grapes for a new arbor. It would look serene, quiet, and faintly pagan. A natural sanctuary. I had liked the descriptions of Roman gardens.

Each evening, Charles and I swam together in his black pool. At first we swam laps. Splashing and churning in parallel lanes, we moved up and down, shamelessly blowing like whales. Or we would breast-stroke beside each other, quietly talking. Out of the water, laughing and dripping, we'd wrap in our robes and sit on the grass. It was hard to leave. I would dress inside and Charles would walk me the six blocks home.

As we continued swimming together each evening, there grew between us an almost palpable silence and calm, like the stillness that comes before high winds and electrical storms. We sat outside and watched the sky darken and the shapes of the trees loom in the night sky. And then Charles would turn off the pool lights and we would slip our white bodies into the black water. We loved moving through its dull bulk, slap, slap, quiet and strange, and the feeling of floating, suspended and buoyant, our pale bodies glowing like large phosphorescent sea creatures.

On the day that the new garden was finished, I found a Georgetown gallery for my Freer drawings. They would mount my show in March. To celebrate, I went down to Muth's, on F Street, and bought a stack of Bristol boards and two dozen sheets of hundred-percent-rag paper. On the way home I stopped at an appliance store on M Street and ordered a dehumidifier for my studio room. It was suddenly clear that I'd be working at home, taking free-lance medical jobs and doing more of my own drawings. I was becoming like Charles; one thing would not be enough.

I came home from my errands to find Matt standing at my front door, his face pale beneath his tan. He took hold of my arm. "Why?" he demanded.

I thought he was talking about my apartment. I detached my arm and unlocked the door. "I need a place of my own," I said. We walked inside.

Matt looked around and then spoke slowly and deliberately, his skin taut over his face. He waved his hand at my apartment in dismissal. "You come with me. You don't need that foreign prick."

Matt must have seen Charles walking me home. Matt must

have seen my face lit up. And Charles's too, a pale fire, his dark eyes burning. I put down my packages and portfolio and turned to face him.

"Don't you remember Venice?" he said. "The beach? All those pictures that everyone saw?"

"Of course I remember. I wished for years—"

"Don't wish!" He sat down on my only chair.

I felt my face hot and heard my voice loud. "Why not wish? What's wrong with wishing?" I stood in front of him, at that moment wanting to see him slumped on the floor, as passive and quiet as he'd been all these years. I took a deep breath. "It's over," I said. I waved my arms. "You had your chance. I loved you for years."

"You don't understand," he said. "Don't you see that you're just like your mother? Chasing the neighbors?"

I stared at him for a long moment. His look was triumphant.

"What do you mean, 'chasing the neighbors'? Explain that."

Matt was silent. The room around us was cool and still, the only sound the white hum of the air conditioner.

I suddenly knew. I didn't have to be told. "There were more letters. You didn't send them all."

"I burned them," he said. He stared at the floor. Then he looked up. "But it's still true. You're just like her."

"You're wrong," I said. I didn't care about letters. I didn't care what my mother had done, whom she'd loved, or why. It no longer mattered. I'd stopped living that way. I said it again: "I'm not my mother. You're quite wrong." He couldn't hear me.

"Leave," I said. He sat where he was, his face impassive.

"You don't understand," he repeated. "You're not able."

"Now," I said. I went to the door and yanked it open. His face looked blank. After a very long time, Matt got up and walked to the door.

People don't change. But with great effort, they sometimes become more true to themselves. Simply more honest.

All my life I'd felt mysteries, inconsistencies, things not right. I'd told myself that mysteries were like scientific problems, a form of question to which answers could, of course, be found. I'd looked for answers in the lab. I'd looked for a solution with Matt. But my family was not a matter of answers. No final understanding would come by learning the relations of the parts, the mother and the father, how they knew each other, what they felt for each other, what they did to each other and if it was good or bad. It was no longer a matter of explanation, of dissection, the endless asking of *Why*, *Why*, the finding of evidence, the analysis of parts and sections and details, the taking of statements from different parties. It was no longer an unraveling enterprise. There were no usable facts or answers. It had changed. It had deepened.

My parents' world was a locked box. I had spent most of my life reacting to its contents, when, all the while, the box was not only locked, but empty; I had filled it with my own inventions. What could be known about others would always be fiction.

There was no mystery. There was only myself.

I followed Matt out to the sidewalk and watched him disappear down the street. I stood for a few minutes in the dusty twilight that comes on early-fall evenings just before dark. The light was draining out slowly, everything was darkening and closing in. The sky lowered, the horizon contracted, and there was for a moment a sense of being outside the ordinary sequence of things—as if weather itself had lost its bearings. Green was still green, but orange glowed behind it, and the sidewalks were littered with acorns and leaves. Instead of the chatter of spring, birds called in long, low, singular notes. Against an off-white sky, cicadas sounded a constant chorus of low-toned sleigh bells. Something had begun, a dissolution, a falling apart and down, a crumbling and disappearance. The day felt like change—surely it would either brighten and clear or darken and rain—but unexpectedly, nothing happened.

That evening, as I slipped into the cool hands of the water, Charles's long white body drifted toward me through the slapping waves, as if a whirlpool were drawing us slowly together. We rolled around one another, our bodies sinking and rising, again and again, softly touching. Finally, we dragged our loosened shapes onto the black grass, and lay there listening to each other breathe. Warm air drifted down on our skin, our luminous hands. After a time we went inside.

Later, when I was dressing, and before Charles walked me home, I wanted to look in his eyes and ask what we meant, what he felt, and what he intended, but I didn't ask. Those questions were wrong. And Charles said nothing. Instead, a kind of somnolence rested over everything. A quiet ticking. Waiting. Abeyance.